ELEANOR

CLOVER SPRINGS MAIL ORDER BRIDES 10

RACHEL WESSON

LONDONGATE PUBLISHING

CHAPTER 1

Eleanor Templeton walked down the street trying not to feel despondent. It was her own fault nobody was waiting for her at the train station. She wasn't due to arrive for another week. But she had to leave Boston, she couldn't bear the stares, some of sympathy and some not so pleasant any longer. She made her way toward the church. The priest always lived near the church, so it was as good a point as any.

The town was a lot smaller than she'd expected. Was she mad coming here? Perhaps she should have chosen a bigger city like Chicago where she could have got lost in the crowd. She walked faster, as fast as her skirts would allow her. People—men mainly—were staring at her, making her uncomfortable. She was so busy worrying about the other people, she didn't see the man until it was too late.

"Excuse me, ma'am."

Eleanor sprang back from him as if burnt. She couldn't breathe but stared at his hand still on her arm. He flushed slightly as he took his hand away.

"Apologies, ma'am, I thought you were going to fall."

She made the mistake of looking at his face. His wide blue eyes stared back at her, frank admiration in their depths. He looked concerned as if worried she was going to scream or worse, faint in a heap at his feet. She was made of sterner stuff than that.

"My apologies, sir. I wasn't looking where I was going."

"You're English." He grinned at her. "I'm from London myself. Been in the States a few years now. How is the old country?"

Eleanor bit her tongue wondering how to reply. In England, strangers didn't speak to ladies, particularly if they were alone. But then well brought up young ladies wouldn't be walking down the street without a chaperone.

"Where were you going? You're a stranger to these parts. Maybe I can escort you the rest of your way?" the stranger asked.

"That won't be necessary." Eleanor's cold tone

wiped the smile off his face. She hadn't meant to be rude. She tried to repair the damage. "Thank you for your kind thought."

She saw the church behind him, but before she could move, she heard a voice behind her.

"Morning, Gary. Ma'am."

"Morning, Father Molloy. I would introduce you but I don't know the young lady's name."

Eleanor's stomach heaved. What would the priest think of her standing in the middle of the boardwalk with a strange man? It was hardly a good first impression. She turned to look at him expecting to see censure in his gaze. Instead, she saw a warm smile.

"Good morning, ma'am. You are new to town. Can I be of assistance?"

"Yes, Father, my name is Eleanor Templeton. You were expecting me but not for another week."

"Miss Templeton. Our new teacher. How delightful. Please come with me. I am sure you are gasping for a cup of coffee after your journey. Pity I didn't know you were on the train. I was just at the station myself." Father Molloy smiled at her.

Eleanor stared while the man called Gary laughed.

"I don't think Miss Templeton is used to priests being so nice, Father. She's English and we don't get many like you back in England." Gary turned his focus to her. "It was nice meeting you, Miss Templeton. I look forward to getting to know you better."

With a tip of his hat he was gone, leaving her alone with Father Molloy.

"English? Well, you have come a far distance, haven't you? Come inside and we will get us a nice cup of coffee."

Father Molloy took her bag despite her protests she could carry it and together they walked to his house beside the church. Eleanor had to fight the urge to look behind her to see if Gary was watching. She wondered what his surname was before correcting her train of thoughts. She'd come here to teach. She wasn't interested in anything else.

* * *

GARY WALKED BACK toward the saloon wondering why the young lady was in Clover Springs. He hadn't noticed her until she'd walked into him. He'd been surprised to see the fear and apprehension in her gaze when he looked in her eyes. She was obviously well off. It wasn't just her clothes but her accent spoke of class and breeding. What would make an English woman travel all this way to teach school in a small town like this? He loved living here but it wasn't exactly the type of place one yearned to live in.

He'd met a lot of women in his time—from all walks of life—but nobody had made a first impression like Miss Templeton. She intrigued him which was unusual as he didn't usually have time for women. But then, at the mines, there weren't many decent women around. Some of the men had wives with them but the majority of the workers were single just like him. Unlike him, they liked to blow off steam when they weren't working. They spent their wages in the saloons and houses of ill repute.

Until Dickinson had come and ruined everything, he'd been happy. Dickinson had gone and he had his saloon back, running just the way he liked it but it wasn't the same. He wanted something more. It would be nice to have a wife and in time some children. But with single women rarer than hen's teeth, he wasn't sure that would ever happen.

CHAPTER 2

Father Molloy looked up from his desk to the young woman sitting in front of him. "Your references are wonderful."

"Thank you, Father," she replied politely.

He continued to study her wondering if she would volunteer more about herself, but she just stared back at him. He coughed, trying to buy a couple of minutes. He had to ask her but he wasn't sure how to frame the question without seeming very rude.

"Yes, Father?"

"Sorry, Miss Templeton, but I am rather curious. I am aware of the reputation of Cheltenham Ladies College. I would have thought there were many vacancies for governesses with your credentials in Britain. Why come to America? But more specifically, what brings you to Clover Springs?"

"You advertised for a teacher. I am fully qualified so I applied for the position. You confirmed it yourself by post."

"Yes, I am aware of that. I am just wondering why you came here? A lady with your background and qualifications could find a position most anywhere in the country."

Her look pierced him right through the heart. "I think we both know that is not the truth, Father. I suspect you are trying to be kind."

Kind? Why would she think he was being kind?

"Miss Templeton, we have only just met, and I know it is rather impertinent for me to suggest you trust me when you know nothing about me. I am very fond of our little town. I believe it to be the best place in the world bar Ireland, of course." He laughed but fell silent when she didn't join him. "Please tell me your story."

"Father, do you not read the papers?" she responded tartly.

He didn't retaliate, sensing her rudeness was covering a deep hurt. He waited but she seemed intent on staying silent until he answered.

"Sometimes, but I am not always up to date."

"The reason I accepted the position is quite simple, Father. You were the only one to offer me employment. I guess you did fewer checks than some other people in your situation."

"Checks?" Father Molloy swallowed hard. What had he opened Clover Springs up to now?

"My full name is Eleanor Amelia Templeton. I was raised as the true daughter of Captain James Templeton. He brought me back from the plantation I was born on to be raised in Britain. I suppose he hoped his wealth, position, and reputation would protect me. It did. For some time, in fact, I was accepted. Looking back, I can see there were comments and snide remarks, but I believed people were jealous over my father's close relationship with the Prince of Wales. That acceptance died with him. Grandmamma, well, I guess I shouldn't call her that anymore, had my bags packed and a steamer booked within two weeks of my father's death. Seems I was an embarrassment to my family. Despite my pale skin, I am the daughter of an ex-slave. My father's family do not believe him to be my father and so refuse to recognize me as such."

"I am very sorry for your loss and for your treatment by your family, but I fail to see how that would adversely affect your suitability for employment." Father Molloy coughed wondering how he could put it discretely. "Nobody needs to know your origins if you do not wish them to. You look white."

"Nellie said you would say that." She looked at him sadly. "You know as well as I do, a drop of black blood means you are considered black regardless of appearance."

"Nellie?"

"She is the cook at the house where I stayed . A friend of a friend recommended Mrs. Gantley. I believe she sent some mail order brides out here."

"Oh yes, of course, Nellie. How could I forget that dear old lady? How is she?" Father Molloy asked.

"She is fine. She said to say hello to you. I wasn't going to bring her up to be honest. I didn't want you thinking I was using anyone to secure this position."

"I don't think that at all. I think you would be perfect for this position, Miss Templeton."

"What of the residents?"

"What do you mean?" he asked genuinely confused.

"Will they be as accepting of a colored woman working as a teacher for white children?"

Father Molloy stared at the beautiful young lady sitting in front of him. He could only imagine the pain she was feeling. It was a very cruel world they lived in.

"Nellie didn't tell you everything about Clover Springs, did she? For a start, we have an Indian as our deputy sheriff. Wilma, an ex-slave, runs our orphanage more or less. You could say she runs the town too. She knows just about everyone in it. Believe me, Miss Templeton, your background is nobody's business, whether you decide to share it with people or not. The parents in Clover Springs will be very happy to have someone of your caliber teaching their children. Now where are you staying? With Martha Sullivan at the boarding house?"

"Yes, Father."

"Well, let me walk you back to the boarding house. It isn't far, just past the school up ahead. If I can, I will introduce you to Ellen Higgins, our main school teacher. Laura Kelley is another teacher in the school. Both those ladies work on a part-time basis, or at least, they should as both have young children and neither are fully recovered from their confinement. So, Miss Templeton, you are the answer to Clover Springs' prayers."

They walked through the streets of Clover Springs. He pointed out various buildings to her, all the while wondering what type of man would take his child away from her own people to try and force society to accept her. Being Irish, he wasn't a huge fan of the British upper-classes having observed long ago their disdain for those they considered beneath them.

CHAPTER 3

As he suspected, Miss Templeton was stared at the whole time. He admired the way she walked, straight back and stiff British upper lip as his mentor Father Clarke used to say. He wondered what plantation she had been born on.

"Miss Templeton, the men here stare at every newcomer to town particularly when they are young and attractive women. Please don't be uncomfortable. You will find many of them will approach you with a view to marriage."

She stopped walking turning to look at him. "I don't think these men would want to marry me. Do you, Father Molloy?"

"I suspect you undersell yourself, my dear. Nobody here knows anything about you. You can tell them as little or as much as you like. You will find people in Clover Springs are very accepting."

She looked around, her eyes giving him a brief glimpse of the happy person she must have been before her papa had died. The delighted expression had gone when she turned her focus back to him. Now her eyes were guarded as if she expected an attack at any second.

"I know you believe that but my experiences of people have proved you wrong. People I considered family and close friends turned their back on me as soon as my background became common knowledge." She faltered as her voice trembled. Taking a couple of seconds to stare at the ground, she swallowed delicately before continuing. "Initially, I assumed they knew I was not purely white but they didn't mind so much. They treated me like some sort of exotic flower but they were never unpleasant. That came, only after my grandmamma made my exact origins known." Miss Templeton's eyes blazed. "It is one thing to be an exotic flower, quite another to have been born the daughter of an ex-slave. People accused me of abusing their trust. Me? I was four or five when I left this country. I didn't know anything of my background. Now that Papa is dead, I guess I will never know."

The hurt and anger blazing out of the beautiful brown eyes looking up at him made him sadder than he had been in a long time. People could be vicious. He knew that better than most given what he had seen in his lifetime. But cruelty like that invoked on this innocent young woman made him very angry.

"It will take time but I hope you will learn to trust the people of Clover Springs. I have lived a lot longer than you, and believe me, I have never met a nicer group of people. Sure, we have our challenges but somehow we always overcome them."

"Thank you, Father, for trying to make me feel better but forgive me for saying this. You are a white man living in a white man's world. You belong. I am neither white nor black. I don't." She took a deep breath. "Thank you for seeing me to the boarding house. I will make my own way from here."

"I will see you soon, Miss Templeton. Martha Sullivan will look after you."

Father Molloy walked away slowly, feeling the weight of every sixty-five years of his life bearing down on his shoulders. All his life, he had been fighting injustice. First back in Ireland, then in Tasmania, and now here. Would the fight ever end?

* * *

ELEANOR WATCHED the old man walk back down the street. She was sorry she had spoken to him like she did, but she couldn't believe in a world where her kind were accepted. She was an outcast and the sooner she accepted that, the better.

She looked at the white-washed clapboard building, its windows sparkling in the winter sun. There were flower boxes at either side of the door with a pretty porch around the front of the house. Despite the lack of color—it being February so the flowers hadn't yet bloomed—it looked pretty and inviting. She spotted a small sign saying Sullivan's Boarding House.

She knocked on the front door. It was opened almost immediately by an older woman, her dark hair liberally streaked with grey surrounded an open, friendly face.

"Yes? Can I help you?"

"Mrs. Sullivan? My name is Eleanor Templeton."

"Oh, my dear, I thought you weren't coming for another week. I would have had a bath ready for you after that horrible train journey. But look at me forgetting my manners. Come in, please make yourself at home."

Eleanor couldn't move, suddenly feeling very emotional. This was the third person to be kind to her in the space of one morning. She stared at the woman, whose kindly expression now turned to concern.

"Are you feeling all right, dear? You seem a little…shaken."

Eleanor gave herself a mental talking to. "I am just tired, it was a long journey from Boston."

"I know, not from personal experience but many of the women in the town have told me of their trials during the trip. Please come with me. I will show you to your room. I am sure you could do with a good sleep."

"Thank you for being so kind." Eleanor choked down her tears. It wasn't done for a lady to cry in public.

"What lovely manners you have. It is my pleasure to have such a cultured young lady under my roof. We have been waiting for a new teacher for weeks now. Laura and Ellen are just not well enough to cope with all the young ones. Especially as the school is hopelessly overcrowded since the last lot of orphans arrived."

Eleanor smiled. Her landlady wasn't exactly selling the job of schoolteacher. Mrs. Sullivan must have read her thoughts as she put her hand to her mouth.

"Listen to me. It isn't as bad as all that. The poor orphans are wonderful children. Wilma, she's the lady who runs the orphanage with Ellen and her husband, keeps them in line."

"I am looking forward to getting to know everyone," Eleanor said politely although she was longing for her bed.

"I have put you in a room at the back of the property. You will get more privacy as sometimes the noise from the street can be a little loud. Though it is much better than it used to be now Gary is back in charge at the saloon. You wouldn't have recognized our town a year or so ago when a bad lot came and tried to take over. But the Clover Springs people banded together like usual and fought them off."

Eleanor stared at her landlady. What type of place had she landed in? She followed her landlady up the stairs in silence. Mrs. Sullivan was still chatting.

"Oh, listen to me. I am scaring you off. Clover Springs is a lovely place to live. You will like it here," Mrs. Sullivan said as she pushed the bedroom door open.

To Eleanor's surprise the room was quite large with a comfortable looking bed in one corner. The sheets were crisp white linen with a beautiful quilt over them. There were braided rugs on the floor and although sparsely furnished, everything gleamed. It wasn't the luxury she had left behind her in England but it was welcoming and comforting. She had a feeling she would be happy here. At least until they found out who she really was.

"You will like it, dear, but for now, it's off to bed you go. You look like you could fall asleep on your feet."

"Thank you, Mrs. Sullivan."

"Good night, dear. When you wake up, I will have the water hot and ready for a bath. But for now, just sleep."

"What about your sheets?" Eleanor asked knowing she was dusty from the train.

"They can be washed. Go on. Put your head down and get some shut-eye." Mrs. Sullivan left, closing the door gently behind her.

Eleanor took off her cloak and shoes before lying on the bed. It was as comfortable as it looked. Before long, she was fast asleep.

* * *

MARTHA SULLIVAN WALKED BACK DOWNSTAIRS WONDERING if she should call Doc Erin to examine her new guest. She was pale and tired, probably due to the journey but was there something else wrong with her? She decided to wait and see how the young lady was after a long rest.

CHAPTER 4

Erin looked at her husband, Mick. She couldn't believe they had only been married a week. It seemed so much longer. She was so glad he had persuaded her to change her mind about getting married again. He was nothing like her previous husband. She refused to think about her first marriage. Nothing was going to ruin today. They were heading out to spend the day with Alicia and her husband Aaron. Alicia wanted to discuss the mine to see if they could do anything to improve the health of the miners.

"Alicia has great plans for the mine, doesn't she?" Erin asked Mick.

"Aaron told me about the work she had done to make it safer. I appreciate what she is doing, but don't you think you have enough work in Clover Springs without adding the mine and logging camps on top?" Mick asked, glancing at her as he drove.

"Are you afraid one of the loggers will carry me off?" Erin laughed at the expression in his eyes. She loved teasing him.

"Not a chance of that happening, my darling wife. You are much too feisty and independent for them."

Erin nudged him gently on the arm. "At least you didn't call me stubborn."

"You? Stubborn? Never," Mick said.

She burst out laughing at his sarcasm. He leaned over and kissed her despite the fact they had just pulled up outside Alicia's house.

"Mick, stop that. Someone will see."

"I see the honeymoon period isn't over yet," Alicia said, smiling as she walked toward them. "Thank you so much for coming out to see us. The boys aren't feeling too well, and I was afraid to bring them out into the cold air."

"What's wrong with them? Do they have a fever or a rash?"

"Relax, Doc. They are fine. It just a cold. You can examine them later. But first, you need coffee to help warm you up."

"Just coffee?" Mick sounded like a lost child.

"Maybe some cookies too?" Alicia added, her eyes gleaming with laughter.

"That's more like it. I sure miss Mrs. H's cookies."

"Charming aren't you, Mr. Quinn. My mother-in-law didn't make them. I did," Alicia said, hands on hips pretending to be insulted.

Erin giggled as Mick pretended to be crestfallen at Alicia's words.

"I think you should just give him a drink, Alicia. That will teach him for being rude."

"Where's your husband, Alicia Higgins? I have had enough of mean women today," Mick said, throwing his arms up in mock surrender.

Laughing, the three of them went into the house where Aaron was playing with his boys. Erin examined them quickly and was relieved to see Alicia was right. They had colds but nothing more. Still, she couldn't help being glad they had left Michelle back at the Haven with Lily.

* * *

"AARON and I asked you to visit because we want to tell you something," Alicia said.

Erin looked at her friend's stomach.

"No, it's not that," Alicia said smiling, but Erin saw the smile didn't reach her eyes. She made a mental note to discuss that with Alicia when the men weren't around.

"We were thinking of taking a trip, and we wanted both of you to come along," Alicia said taking her husband's hand in hers.

"Where are you going?" Erin asked.

"New York," Alicia said excitedly. "I have never been. A friend of my father, I used to call him Uncle Randolph when I was little, wrote and invited us to come. He has opened a new hotel and offered us accommodation. I have always wanted to see a show on Broadway but it's never been a good time. But now is perfect. Aaron can't do much around here until it warms up a little. Davy has offered to look after the place for us."

"New York is wonderful. You will have a fantastic time," Erin said, not managing to keep a note of envy from her voice.

"We know but we would love you to come too. Call it a wedding present." At the look on Erin's face, Alicia quickly continued. "Erin, you never let me pay you properly for your work at the mine. You have been so good to me. Please let me share my good fortune with you and your family."

Before Erin or Mick could protest, Alicia continued. "I know you don't want to be away from Michelle so bring her too. Please say you will think about it?"

Erin exchanged a glance with Mick. She wanted to go but what would he think? Like most men, her husband had his pride. Would he accept such an expensive gift?

* * *

MICK WATCHED his wife's face. He knew she missed New York and some of the people she had known while living there. She worried about Mrs. Doherty, her ex-housekeeper, and how she was managing. The older woman had written to say work was scarce. There were also friends of her parents whom she regularly talked about.

There was no way their resources would cover a trip, not after buying the Haven and spending all their money changing it from the former brothel into a respectable residence. He hated taking money from Alicia, but Erin had earned at least some of it. She worked hard up at the mine.

"Mick, please think about it. I am not sure I am capable of going shopping with my wife much as I adore her." Aaron glanced at his wife before staring back at Mick, a pleading look in his eyes. "I hate cities, all those people, all that noise. Denver was bad enough when I went to file the claim for this place with Davy Sullivan. I can't imagine how much worse New York will be. If you were there, it wouldn't be so bad."

Mick stared at Aaron. It was probably the longest

speech he had ever heard him make. He looked at Erin, she was staring back at him, her eyes shining with excitement.

"Thank you very much, Alicia, for your generous offer," he began. Erin coughed as if she expected him to say no. "We would love to accept."

Erin threw her arms around him. "Thank you, darling," she whispered. He squeezed her hand in acknowledgement.

Alicia jumped up and down. "I am like a child on Christmas morning. I am so excited. How does the end of next week suit you both?"

"We will make it work," Erin said, her face lit up with happiness. "Oh, it will be so exciting. Mick, I can show you where I used to work, and, Alicia, I can bring you to the best shops. The children can see the Barnum and Bailey Circus."

"Do you think Lily will come with us? If she does, would she help mind the boys?" Alicia asked. "It would be nice to try some of the fancy restaurants I have heard so much about. I don't like leaving the children with strangers."

"I am sure she would. She doesn't like being away from Michelle," Erin confirmed.

"Wonderful. You must come and help me pack. I don't know what to bring. I guess my dresses are all hideously out of date."

Mick exchanged a look with Aaron.

"Why don't I show you the new horse I bought from Little Beaver. He brought it over yesterday. I am not sure I could leave him so quickly. He won't be used to his new home." Aaron winked at Mick but his wife obviously missed it.

"Don't you start again, Aaron Higgins. You agreed to this trip and you can't go back on your word now."

"I love you, darling, but go pack. Come on, Mick, let's go out to the barn."

"Can we come too, Pa? I hate women's talk," Harry asked.

Mick smothered a laugh at the expression on the young boy's face.

"Not today, son, your ma will have kittens. You have to get rid of that cold before we can go on the train."

"I don't like trains," Steven, Harry's younger brother muttered.

Alicia was by his side almost as soon as the words came out of his mouth. "Darling, it won't be anything like last time. We will have comfortable seats, nice food and nobody will be shouting at you. I promise."

Mick gulped trying to dislodge the lump in his throat. Since when had he become so sentimental? He'd heard of the boys' experiences on the same train Alicia had travelled on from Boston. He watched as the little boy wrapped his arms around Alicia's neck.

"Thanks, Ma."

"Where's this horse?" Mick was getting eager to get some air. He hated being reminded of past tragedy involving young children. It always made him think of his sisters.

* * *

"THANK you so much for saying yes," Erin said snuggling into her husband's arm as they traveled home. It was cold and she was looking forward to getting home and seeing her daughter.

"Do you think Doc will be able to cope?" Mick asked. "He missed you when you were away studying."

"I don't think he will mind. It will only be for two weeks. Mrs. Grey and Mrs. Shipley are here to help." Erin glanced up at him. "Are you saying you have changed your mind?"

"No. I wouldn't do that. But, well…it doesn't sit right, the Higgins spending all that money on us."

Erin went to talk but changed her mind realizing he hadn't finished.

"I know how much you want to go back and see everyone. I totally understand you wanting to show those old fogies you did it. You became a real doctor."

"Childish of me I know but...well, I can't help it."

"It's perfectly understandable." Mick gave her a quick hug with one hand. "I will go with you, although you might want to leave the room when I thank them."

"Thank them? Why would you do that?" Erin asked, totally mystified.

"For being so ignorant, judgmental and downright old fashioned. If it hadn't been for them, I would never have met you."

Erin giggled as she snuggled closer. "I guess I should thank them too."

CHAPTER 5

"Doc Erin, do you have a minute?"

Erin looked up from the periodical she had been reading to see Karl, the logger who was helping run the mill while waiting for his arm to heal. Seeing him reminded her she should visit the logging camp when she got back from her vacation. She had caught up on everything in preparation for her trip to New York and was now relaxing. "Come in please, Karl. How is your arm? Are you in pain?"

"No, not in pain. Not from arm anyway. I is, I mean I would like to... This is difficult." Karl twisted his hat around his fingers. Erin had to hide her smile, the hat wouldn't be fit to wear if he worked it so hard for much longer.

"Karl, sit down please and take a deep breath. Now

tell me where it hurts," Erin said using her most soothing doctor's voice.

"In here." Karl pointed to his chest. "I think... My heart, it is broken."

It took Erin a couple of minutes to work out Karl wasn't looking for medical advice.

"Karl, are you trying to tell me you are in love?"

"Ya. Ya. With woman."

Erin smiled, waiting but he just continued to stare at her. "Karl, which woman? And why do you need my help?"

"Mrs. Hofmeister. She is fine woman. And baby Mia is beautiful little girl. I like Max too," Karl supplied.

"So what's the problem?" Erin asked, wondering how many male doctors found themselves consulted in matters of the heart.

"Mrs. Hofmeister no like you. She real stubborn. She want to go live in other place. I want to stay here. Good business in the mill and good friends in town."

Erin hid her smile behind her hand. Who would have thought someone wouldn't think she was stubborn? That was one to tell her husband, Mick. What was she supposed to do? She wasn't well versed in matters of the heart having only recently allowed herself to trust the man she loved with every bone in her body. She looked helplessly at Karl.

"Karl, I fixed your arm when you hurt it at the logging camp. I don't think..."

"Yes, you fixed arm real good. So now you fix heart too. Yes?"

"But..."

"Mrs. Hofmeister listens to you. She think you have big brain. You tell her marry me." Karl stood up, his head nodding so fast, Erin grew dizzy. She stood up too.

"Well, I can try speaking to her. It hasn't been that long since she lost her husband." The accident at the mill had happened the first day Erin arrived in town. She would never forget Hans Hofmeister for as long as she lived. The poor man had been so brave, even when she had to amputate his arm. She still wondered if she could have done anything to save him. He'd left a pregnant widow and young son devastated.

"It's been almost one year. I lost my wife two years now. My girl needs mother. Mrs. Hofmeister needs father for two children. It's perfect, yes?"

Erin just stared at him. She wished someone else was here to help. Mrs. Grey was out checking on some patients and Emer Shipley had gone home to her beautiful twins.

"You come now and talk. Take no time." Karl held her cloak out for her. "Now, please."

Erin found herself agreeing. The smile on his face was worth it.

* * *

THEY SOON ARRIVED at the mill. Erin asked Karl to wait outside leaving her to talk to Mrs. Hofmeister in private. The widow was nursing her little girl, immediately making Erin think of Michelle. She missed her adopted daughter when she was working. Lily looked after her really well, but she couldn't help being a little bit jealous. Mick wouldn't mind if she stopped doctoring to stay home all day with Michelle. But much as she hated to admit it, she wouldn't find that satisfying. She loved being a doctor. Well, most days anyway.

"Good afternoon, Mrs. Hofmeister. How are you and Mia today?"

"We are good but you call me Greta, please. You are my friend." Mrs. Hofmeister beamed at Erin making her feel worse. How much of a friend would she think she was after she put forward Karl's proposal?

"Greta, I was wondering, I mean as your doctor, I thought I would check on your plans."

"My plans?" Greta looked confused.

"You said before Mia came, you wanted to go to

Kansas to be with your friends. Are you still planning to move?"

Disappointment flooded Greta's face, leaving Erin completely confused.

"Yes, we go. We not stay long here."

"But why?" Erin asked gently.

"Why?"

"Why are you going? Dickinson is gone—he was hanged last month for Kathryn's murder among others. So why leave?" Erin asked.

Confusion replaced disappointment in the other woman's eyes. "You not tell me to leave?"

Erin wasn't often lost for words but this time Mrs. Hofmeister succeeded. Erin tried again. "Greta, we would love if you, Max, and baby Mia stayed in Clover Springs. Karl is a fine man. He would like to stay here too. He doesn't want to go back to the logging camp."

Greta stopped nursing and took her time to readjust her clothing. Then she stood up and put baby Mia into the cradle.

"That's a beautiful cradle, Greta."

Greta touched the cradle, a smile on her lips. "Karl make it. He is good man but people talk. They say it too soon. After my Hans."

Erin wished people would mind their own business. It seemed there was always someone telling someone else what they could and couldn't do.

"Greta, never mind about anyone else. What do you feel? Do you think it is too soon?"

Greta shook her head but she wouldn't meet Erin's eyes.

"Tell me, please. I am your friend and your doctor. I won't say a word to anyone else."

"I think it would be nice to be a real family again. It is hard being mother and father to the children at same time. Max needs a father. He is growing boy."

"Karl would make a good father. But what about you? What do you want?"

Greta flushed. "I think Karl make good husband."

"Well then, please say you will stay. If you like, you could start courting Karl. That would give people time to get used to the idea, although if I was you, I would just get married. Life is far too short to worry about what other people think."

"What other people?" Greta was confused again.

Erin would have smiled but she didn't want to offend the lady.

"Greta, do what you think is best about Karl. Now there is something else I wanted to ask you. Would you come to English classes if I could organize some?"

"English classes?"

"Your English is very good but sometimes you find it hard to understand people. Or they misunderstand you. We have a lot of new people in Clover Springs. I was thinking I might start some English classes for the adults."

"You could make me speak like you? That would be wonderful." Greta nodded so hard, Mia protested with a wail. "Shush little one. Mama wants you to grow up American. I need to speak good English so I can teach children."

Erin stood up, pleased to have had such a successful visit.

"Thank you, Doc Erin."

"Can I please tell Karl to come and speak to you. I think the poor man will eat his own hat, he is so nervous."

Greta smiled as she raised her head shyly. Erin glimpsed the beauty she must have been before the worries of the last few years had made her careworn.

"You tell Karl to come talk," Greta said in her broken English.

"I will. Goodbye, little Mia. See you soon, Greta. Don't forget to invite me to your wedding."

Erin went out the door smiling. Karl was pacing up and down the street outside.

"Did she listen?" Karl asked.

"Why don't you go inside and ask your fiancée?"

Karl looked at her, confusion in his eyes. At Erin's wide smile, the confusion disappeared to be replaced by a look of sheer delight, it took Erin's breath away.

Before she knew what was happening, Karl lifted her up as if she was a small child and swung her around. She was breathless when he put her back on the ground. “Sorry, Doc. I got excited. Thank you.” He moved inside quickly, closing the door behind him.

“Did I just see you being manhandled in the street?” Mick said, the grin on his face showing her he had seen the innocence in Karl's embrace.

“I've decided to give up doctoring and take up matchmaking instead.” Erin leaned in for a kiss from her husband. She couldn’t believe how much she enjoyed being married. Mick hadn't changed into a beast as soon as he put the ring on her finger. In fact, he was more patient and happier in himself. Marriage suited them both. They knew they had been blessed to adopt Michelle even though it wasn’t formal yet. Their little girl meant their family was complete.

* * *

SHE LINKED his arm as they walked down the street.

“Erin, you know what you said about matchmaking?”

“I wasn’t serious, you know.”

“I know that and anyway the town wouldn’t let you stop doctoring but you could still be a matchmaker in your spare time.”

"Who do you want to marry off? Lily? I don't think she is ready yet do you?"

No, he didn't, and if he was honest, he wasn't sure she would ever be. It was such a shame as the more they got to know Lily the more he liked her. She was a victim of Dickinson just as much as Mollie, Kathryn, and the others. But because she was over eighteen she didn't get the same sympathy. It was stupid as Dickinson had entrapped her as a thirteen-year-old runaway.

"No, it's not Lily, although I wish it was. I was thinking of Cookie and Mrs. H."

Erin stopped right in the middle of the street. "You want me to set up your best friend with your old housekeeper?"

"Well, Davy's housekeeper but yeah."

"Ha. I am not that good. Mrs. H has been widowed for years. If she wanted to get married, she would have done so already. It's not like there aren't plenty of single men around. Cookie has never been interested in settling down. I am not a miracle worker."

Mick didn't respond, he just looked at her.

"You're serious, aren't you?"

"Yes, dear wife, I am. Not just because you have shown me the joys of wedded bliss, but I really care for both of them, and I think they will make a good match. I owe Cookie a lot."

Erin rubbed his arm. “Cookie doesn’t see it like that. You don't have to pay him for looking out for you. He says you are the son he never had.”

“Well, maybe now he could have children of his own.”

Erin laughed but stopped at his expression. “Mick Quinn, do I have to explain the facts of life to you? Mrs. H is too old to have a baby, and I am not at all sure she would want one after all these years.”

“Not her own baby but I think she would make a wonderful mother to some orphans.”

“Ah, why didn't I think of that?”

“Because you, my darling wife, are not always the best at seeing the obvious.”

He brushed her lips lightly only showing restraint because they had reached the clinic and the room inside was bound to be occupied by patients. “See you for dinner.”

CHAPTER 6

Mick walked on down to the Haven. The property had been completely transformed inside and out. There was no resemblance now to the Red Feathers. Little Beaver and some of the other men had helped him plant a row of trees between the saloon and the Haven to make sure everyone knew the properties were not linked.

Mick rubbed his chin as he passed the saloon, thinking of Gary the barkeep.

It was about time Gary settled down and met a nice woman. Mick chuckled loudly making the man walking down the street toward him, cross to the other side. Who would have thought a year ago he would be matchmaking all his friends? He, who had been a confirmed bachelor, was now trying to get everyone married off.

"You seem in a very happy mood," Lily said as Mick walked into the Haven still chuckling.

"I am, Lily. How's Michelle?"

Lily's face lit up. "She's asleep now, the little angel. She is such a beautiful child. I can't understand how her father let her go."

"Neither can I but I am so thankful he did." Mick turned his attention away from the crib back to Lily. "How are you? How was your day?"

The smile slid off her face faster than ice melting in the summer sun. He thought she was about to cry, but instead, she took a deep breath. "It was same as always."

"Lily, remember what we promised each other when you decided to live here with me and Erin? No lies."

"I took Michelle to the store. I shouldn't have. I should know better." Lily crossed her arms across her chest.

"Lily, come into the kitchen and sit down. I'm starving. I will make us both some lunch."

Lily laughed. "I am not that upset. I will make lunch, you can make the coffee."

Mick took his lead from her and pretended to be upset. "Are you saying I am a bad cook?"

"Let me see. Before you came here, Cookie did all the cooking for you. Unless Mrs. H was around.

Before that you ate army rations. You never really got the chance to learn."

"Now listen here, miss, you take that back. I can make a decent…" Mick couldn't keep it up. She was right. He was particularly useless in the kitchen. "Okay, you win. I will make the coffee. I can't burn that."

"Well, you would think not but you could." Lily said teasing him back, her eyes letting him know she was grateful to him for lightening the atmosphere.

She would tell him what happened in town when she was ready. He had the time to wait. Erin had taught him a lot of things. They included never to try rushing a lady. With everything Lily had been through, he needed to take things slowly. Difficult to do when his first instinct was to throttle whomever had hurt her earlier today. She had been hurt enough to last a lifetime.

"Lily, are you ready to tell me what upset you today?" Mick asked.

She looked up wondering if she could distract him. She knew he was going to be upset if she told him the truth but then she had promised never to lie to him or Erin. She ran her fingers along the counter.

"I took Michelle to the store. Usually, it's only Katie or Daniel Sullivan in there. They are both nice. But yesterday I got lucky."

"Who?"

"Mrs. Kelley, Mrs. Shaw, and someone else."

"A younger woman?"

Lily nodded. "Mrs. Kelley started making comments about the air smellin' bad. Katie told her to shush but it made no difference. She kept on saying nasty things until I left."

"You were right to leave, Lily. Nobody should have to listen to Ma Kelley. Her son and daughter-in-law won't have anything to do with her."

"I know but that's not why I left. I got so angry I could have slapped her. Sheriff told me I had to stay out of trouble, but it was almost worth sitting in a cell just to have wiped that smug look off her face."

Mick laughed at the sight of Lily making a fist with her hand. He stopped at the look she gave hm.

"It will never stop, will it? People don't forget. There isn't a future for me here in Clover Springs. My own brother wrote me off. Why did I expect ordinary people to treat me better?"

Mick would have given her a hug but it was not appropriate. He was a married man and she was a single woman, not a family member.

"Lily, it is easy for me to tell you things will get better with time. But I don't know if that is true. People do have long memories. But you know Erin and I would do anything to help you."

"What are we doing now?" Erin walked in the front door. She was smiling but then she must have sensed the atmosphere. She dropped her bag and went to Lily straight away.

"You're upset? Why?"

Lily couldn't answer so Mick filled Erin in on what happened at the store.

"I could strangle that woman. She never opens her mouth to say anything nice." Erin responded angrily.

"Mollie wrote me. She writes nice letters. She likes living in Santa Fe."

"Do you want to go live with Mollie?"

"Part of me would but what about Michelle? I mean, I know you can replace me but she might miss me."

"Lily, Michelle will also know about you. You can write to her and we can take her to Santa Fe someday to visit you and Mollie. I don't want you to leave. But more than that, I want you to be happy. If that means you have to go to Santa Fe, then that's what you should do."

Erin hugged Lily. "We will miss you dreadfully but like Mick says, we want you to be happy."

"I think I would like to leave then, please. I know I am running away but..."

"You are not running away, dear girl. You are young enough to start over. Just like Mollie did."

"I don't think I am cut out for school."

"No, probably not, but I am sure Harriet, Wilma's friend, has good contacts and will help you get a job. We will give you an excellent reference. You are brilliant with young children."

Mick nudged Erin.

"Oh my, I almost forgot. Would you delay your departure for a few weeks?"

"Of course I can. I don't want to leave you but…"

Erin hugged the younger girl. "I know you don't and it's not what we want either but a fresh start may be just what you need. But, we would love you to come on vacation with us first. We are going to New York."

Lily's mouth fell open.

"It's true. I am going home for a couple of weeks thanks to Alicia. I can't wait to go into the hospital and show those pompous men I am finally a real and respectable doctor."

Mick put his arm around her. "You were always respectable. They were just too blind to see a good thing when they had it. I should thank them. If they weren't so biased, we wouldn't have met."

"Do you really want me to come? Wouldn't you prefer to go alone?"

The uncertainty in Lily's eyes nearly had Erin in tears. The poor girl had been through so much already. She couldn't believe something nice was going to happen to her. Erin resolved to pamper her as much as she could on their trip.

"We are certain, aren't we, Mick?"

"Sure. We aren't going alone. It's not like a real honeymoon. Alicia, Aaron and their boys are going. You and Michelle are coming with us."

"I'm going to take Michelle up for her nap and write to Mollie. Thank you."

They both watched her as she walked up the stairs toward her room. They knew despite the way she held her head up, inside she was devastated at the thought of leaving Clover Springs for good.

"I would love to give Ma Kelley a shove off a cliff."

Mick put his arm around his wife. "Please don't do that. You might hurt the cliff."

Erin looked at him before she burst out laughing. "I am so glad I found you Mr. Quinn."

"I am glad I married you and know better than to get on the wrong side of your temper," Mick responded pulling her into a deep hug. She went to say something but he silenced her with a kiss, pushing all thoughts of everything else out of her head.

CHAPTER 7

Gary Barrett cleaned the counters and the floor ready for opening time, his thoughts on the young lady he had met yesterday. He wondered what she was doing in Clover Springs? More to the point, who had hurt her so badly, she'd looked scared to death when he spoke to her.

Gary liked everything to be neat and tidy. The men didn't appreciate it, they probably didn't even notice but he did. He always cleaned when he had things on his mind. He liked his job but after the incident with Dickinson and his men, he wasn't as comfortable as he once was. There had to be a better way of making a living than selling alcohol, especially as he never touched the stuff himself. He didn't realize he was scrubbing so hard at a particularly bad stain until a customer interrupted him.

"You are just like an old woman the way you keep this place so clean. Could eat your dinner off the floor you could."

"Whiskey, Murph?"

"Aye, and make it a large one. Been a bad day."

Gary smiled to himself. It was just after noon so the day couldn't have been that long or that bad. Murph was relatively new to Clover Springs. He had worked in the mines all his life until the dust got to his chest. Someone suggested he come to Clover Springs for the air. Doc Erin wasn't too hopeful about his recovery which was a pity as he was a nice enough fella if you could get past his whining.

"You should get yourself a wife. Get her to do all the scrubbing. Not right to see a man working like that."

"I wouldn't mind a wife but I wouldn't want her just for scrubbing. My mum showed me how to keep a house smart," Gary retorted.

"Did she not have lots of children to keep her busy? That's what a woman needs. Keeps them out of trouble."

Gary grinned despite the fact Murph wasn't trying to be funny. He would love to see what Doc Erin thought of Murph's way of thinking.

"No, it was just the two of us. Dad died. In an explosion."

"In the mines, was it?"

"No, back in London. We lived in Clerkenwell."

"Are you trying to tell me you're related to Michael Barrett? The poor auld innocent devil those English bas..."

"Murph, I'm English."

Murph glared at him while taking a large gulp of his drink. "Forgot you were one of them. Although have to say you're quite nice for an English fella."

Gary didn't react. He believed Murph meant no harm.

"So how come you got caught up in the explosion?"

"We lived beside the prison. When they blew a hole in the wall, it brought down nearly half our street. My dad was caught in it. My mum had taken me to the shops."

"Right eejits they were. Knew nothing about explosives. Supposed to blow a small hole in the wall and instead they nearly blew the whole of London up. Good job they didn't work on our mines. We'd all be in kingdom come."

Gary didn't answer. Murph was good at talking to himself.

"They hanged an innocent man for that. Same name as you come to think of it. Any relation?"

"Murph, I told ya. I'm English."

"Oh yeah, forgot. You're too nice to be English."

Murph repeated himself as was the habit with drunks. "Sure you weren't adopted?"

When Gary didn't answer, Murph asked. "How come you ended up here? You seem healthy enough."

Gary smiled. Murph seemed to think most people had come to Clover Springs for health benefits. Doc Erin said there was some benefit to living in a small town compared to a big city where the air was smokier.

"My mum had family in Leadville. They paid for the ship passage. She kept house for my uncle. He worked in the mines and used the money he made to buy a saloon. He didn't have any children. He showed me the ropes. Said he didn't want me going down the mines for the rest of my life."

"Right too he was. I wish I'd done the same for my lads. They might still be alive. But I was always too fond of this stuff," Murph took a large gulp and indicated Gary should refill his glass. "How did you end up here?"

"I worked the mines for a while, saved every cent and bought this place."

"You did well getting out of the mines."

Gary didn't answer. He nodded to Father Molloy as the priest came through the door.

"Afternoon, Gary. Murph."

"Father Molloy. I was just having a wee drink to wet my whistle. I wasn't going to stay all day."

"Sure, it's up to you what you do, Murph. I am not your mother."

"My mother was a fine woman. She didn't take no sh—notice of anyone," Murph corrected himself quickly remembering the presence of the priest. "When those English animals came to turn her out of her home, she stood in the doorway. They had to lift her out… A fine woman she was. Everyone said so."

Father Molloy exchanged a look with Gary. They both had heard the story more than once. Gary believed Murph must have a bottle of liquor stored in his lodgings as he was far too well gone after just a glass and a bit.

"Did you want a drink, Father?"

"No thank you, lad, bit early for me. I was after a favor."

"Unusual for you, Father," Gary said sarcastically but he smiled to show he was joking.

Father Molloy ignored his sarcasm giving him a gentle smile. Gary could see why the people of Clover Springs loved this man so much. Gary never went to church. His family was Protestant but nobody went to services apart from his mother at Christmas. He'd been brought up to distrust any member of the Catholic church but this man was different. He was the only Irish man he'd ever discussed the British and Irish problem with and not ended up in a fist fight. Father Molloy believed passionately in a free Ireland but he didn't condone violence to achieve their aims. Unlike Murph, he didn't blame every English person for the actions of the British government and their representatives in Ireland. Back in Leadville, some people seemed to hold Gary personally responsible for the Irish famine.

"What can I do for you, Father?"

"I was hoping you would help us organize the house raising for the orphanage. We desperately need more space. The poor children are sleeping on every conceivable space."

"Pleasure, Father. I would donate a couple of bottles of the hard stuff to keep the lads warm while working but I think Mrs. Grey and Wilma might have me hauled over the coals for that."

"I guess they would but I am sure some of the men would welcome a drop or two. Davy Sullivan might have a suggestion on that front. So can I count on you?"

"Yes, Father."

Gary waited as the priest seemed to have something else on his mind. What the priest said next surprised him.

"Do you know how to dance?"

"Yes, Father, but I don't dance with priests."

"Be away with you, Gary Barrett. You should have more respect talking to a man of the cloth like that," Murph protested loudly.

"He's a man like the rest of us with a good sense of humor."

Murph ignored him, his wavering gaze now trying to focus on Father Molloy.

"Will you have women at this dance, Father?"

"Of course, Murph. Everyone will have worked hard all day so the dance later will be their reward." Father Molloy gave Murph a stern look. "You might want to clean yourself up a bit if you are trying to impress a lady."

"Not for me. I hung my boots up long ago. For this young man, here. Even if he is English." Murph pointed to Gary as if there was another person in the bar. "Father, did you know he's English? I reckon he was adopted. He's too nice to be one of those heathens."

"Stan Murphy, that's enough of that. I think it's time you went home and slept it off." Father Molloy's steely tone seemed to cut through the fog of Murph's drunken state. With a sigh, the old man finished his drink and headed out the door.

Gary had to turn away to hide his amusement. Father Molloy could be strict and scary when necessary. Looking at him now, you would never guess he had been joking and laughing a few minutes previously.

"Thank you, Father, but Murph is harmless. He doesn't mean what he's saying."

"Unfortunately, Gary, he means every word. There are plenty of my countrymen who think the same way. Until people recognize we are all just people, regardless of where we were born, our religion, or the color of our skin, the world will never find peace."

Gary listened but didn't say anything. He had a feeling Father Molloy wasn't just talking about Murph. Someone else had upset him. He racked his brains wondering who. He hadn't seen the usual suspects in town. Charlie Staunton and his friends, Mrs. Shaw and Ma Kelley could upset anyone.

He decided to try to distract the priest. "Who else is helping, Father?"

"Quite a few of the men thankfully. Davy, Mick, Little Beaver..."

"Father Molloy, I've been looking for you everywhere," Mick said as he walked into the saloon. "Wasn't really expecting to find you in here though."

"Mick Quinn, I have just been talking about you." Father Molloy beamed at the new arrival.

"I hope it was all nice, although you are going to be cross now."

"Why?"

"I'm going to New York. Erin, Michelle and Lily are going too."

"You need a holiday but New York? It's miles away, and at this time of year. It's a bit sudden, isn't it?" Father Molloy asked.

"Yes, I know, Father, but it's our honeymoon. It's Erin's old home. She has people she wants to see, old friends and neighbors. Alicia has been invited and she extended the invite to us."

"So Aaron Higgins is off gallivanting too. Who is going to help me with the extension on the orphanage?"

"I will, but can we put it back until later in the year? The weather will be warmer. Say early April or whenever Easter falls this year?"

"That's an excellent idea, Mick. It makes sense, Father. You will have more volunteers, too, as the men can come in from the outlying homesteads," Gary added keen to avoid a confrontation between his two friends.

"True. I can't argue with the pair of you. I best go and tell Wilma. Oh, she is going to be cross."

"Tell her she can always use the Haven in the meantime. There are plenty of rooms going begging and we won't be there for the next two weeks."

Father Molloy slapped Mick hard on the back.

"Wonderful idea. Why didn't I think of that? Good day, gentlemen."

Mick and Gary watched the priest as he walked out of the saloon.

"New York? I sure wouldn't mind seeing that place," Gary said wistfully.

CHAPTER 8

"Afternoon, Wilma." Father Molloy pushed open the door of the orphanage kitchen. "Have you warmed up yet after our wait at the train station yesterday?"

"Did you smell the coffee? I swear as soon as the pot starts boiling, it sings your name." Wilma made them both coffee before sitting down at the table. Father Molloy had already made himself at home, munching away at one of her cookies.

"I came to tell you we have to postpone the house raising, seems the whole of Clover Springs is off to New York next week."

"I ain't goin' to New York."

"Alicia and Aaron are going with their boys and they are taking Doc Erin, Mick, Michelle and Lily. The town will seem empty without them, won't it?"

"You is an ole softy, ain't you? I am sure they won't stay away too long."

"About two weeks, I believe. Anyway, Mick suggested we wait until Easter to put on the extra rooms to this place. Can you wait till then?"

Wilma smiled. She could definitely wait. The thought of all the hard work and mess associated with building made her tired today. "It don't seem that long since this orphanage was built and its already too small to cover our needs."

"Before you say it, I know," Father Molloy said.

"You know what?" She eyed him.

"I am to blame. I was the one who brought you the extra orphans."

"Really? I thought that was Alicia's fault. I done tole her it was too," Wilma said grinning at the priest. "You is Catholic. You already feel guilty for everything. Might as well spread it around."

"Wilma, that's a dreadful thing to say to a priest."

"Why? It's the truth, isn't it? I read the good book like you tole me too. I don't see where it says in there you have to feel guilty all the time. Maybe it's an Irish thing rather than a catholic thing."

"You know, Wilma, I thank God every day since I met you. You make the world a richer place."

Wilma frowned. "Why you being so nice to me? What you gone and done now?"

"Nothing. At least not that I know of. I was just being pleasant."

"Hmph. I don't believe you. And don't give me that I am a priest so I can't lie lark. You is up to something. You got a twinkle in your eye."

"Well, I do need a favor now that you mention it."

"See, I knew it. You never did come here just to see me. You wants something, just like always."

Father Molloy roared laughing. "You know, Wilma, you don't look a bit like my mam, God rest her soul, but you would be her twin. She used to scold me in that same tone of voice too."

"I ain't scolding you. I just tellin' ya, you shouldn't beat around the bush with me. Who is in trouble this time?"

"Wilma, nobody is in trouble but someone may need a little help adapting to Clover Springs. I have found us a new teacher."

Wilma beamed, her smile almost splitting her face. "About time too. I tole you Miss Ellen and Miss Laura were still too sick to mind that school all by themselves. So where did your teacher come from? Why don't you introduce her to the educated ladies like Miss Ellen and Doc Erin?"

"She's from England, at least that is where she traveled from. I will introduce her to everyone but… Well, I feel Miss Templeton is going to need a good friend in the coming weeks. Someone to help her settle down into our town. There is no better person than you."

"Father Molloy, what ain't you tellin' me? There has to be something wrong with her if you ain't asking Miss Ellen or Miss Laura to show her the ropes. They be working with her." Wilma sighed. "I got a lot on my plate at the moment with all the orphans and Lily and this house. I just ain't sure I got the energy to be someone's else's friend right now." Wilma stared at the table unable to look him in the eyes. She knew she would see disappointment and shock. She had never turned away anyone before but she was tired. Real tired and homesick and lonesome. She couldn't put that into words. How did you tell your closest friends you were lonely without hurting them?

She almost jumped through the ceiling when she felt his hand on hers. He patted it gently as if willing her to say something. He stayed silent, waiting.

She kept her mouth closed firmly. She was tempted to tell him what was on her mind. How scared she was of getting older and sicker. Would she die before she got the chance to make things right?

"Wilma, I apologize. I have been very selfish and you are quite right to be cross with me. I do expect a lot from you and you are only one person. I am sorry I have added to your burden. I will find someone else."

Overwhelmed with shame, she risked glancing at

him. There was only compassion and perhaps concern in his eyes. No censure. She swallowed hard.

"Don't mind me, Father, I just got out of bed on the wrong side this morning. What do you need?"

She kept swallowing at the look of relief in his face. There was no backing out now.

"Let me refill our cups and then you can tell me all about this new teacher of yours."

She went to the stove using the couple of minutes of silence to compose herself. Taking a seat once more, she waited for him to start his story.

"Miss Templeton is highly qualified. She holds excellent references from a rather splendid school in Britain. She is well educated, has lovely manners and is obviously from a cultured background."

"So what's the problem? She don't sound like she needs no help."

"Her family just disowned her."

"Why? What she do?"

Father Molloy looked at her, his eyes full of sadness. "Wilma, I am worried about you. You look like my friend, you even scolded me like she does but now you sound nothing like her. I have never known you to assume someone did something before. Can't you tell me what is wrong? I've been told I am a good listener."

Wilma stared at him. She knew he was the kindest,

most generous spirited person she had ever come across but could she tell him? Would he still look at her the same way? Would he still be her friend if he knew the truth? She fought with herself as he sat waiting, his expression willing her to trust him. She almost felt she could but it was too big a risk.

"I'm sorry, Father. I didn't sleep well. Doc Erin gave me some new pills and they give me bad dreams. Please tell me about Miss Templeton. I promise to be nice."

"Miss Templeton's father, or at least the man she believed to be her father died recently."

"Oh, the poor girl. But you said her family threw her out."

"They did more than that. They disowned her. Her grandmother told her she was no longer a part of the family. She bought her a one-way ticket to America. She ended up staying with Mrs. Gantley, the woman who sent Katie here as a mail-order bride. She sounds English, but she's American by birth. Born somewhere down South."

Wilma's heart beat faster. She didn't want to know the answer to her next question. She couldn't speak, the room was too hot and her breathing was too fast. She saw Father Molloy's mouth open, he was saying something but she couldn't hear him the roaring in her ears was too loud. She'd known that someday the ghosts of the past would come to collect their dues. Was that why her sleep has been so disturbed? Had she sensed them coming. Ole Granny used to say the spirits could find you no matter how far you ran and how long you hid. Her head started spinning so she put it on the table.

"Wilma, drink this slowly," Father Molloy said not quite hiding the panic in his voice. "John, go fetch Doc Erin, tell her to come quickly. Then go and get Mick and Samuel if you can find them. Go now."

"Is Miss Wilma sick? She looks funny."

"Go, John, the sooner you bring the doc back, the better Wilma will be."

Wilma heard this going on in the background. She tried to speak but nothing came out. She went to take a sip of water but her hand was shaking so much, the water splashed everywhere. What was happening to her? The darkness descended slowly. She squeaked, "forgive me, Father," before she passed out.

CHAPTER 9

Doc Erin spotted the stranger walking past the clinic. She stepped outside. "Miss Templeton?"

Startled to hear her name, Eleanor turned back to see a woman running toward her, her skirt held above her ankles.

"Forgive me for startling you but I wanted to say hello and welcome you to Clover Springs. My name is Erin Quinn but most call me Doc Erin. I met Martha Sullivan at the store and she said you were resting after your long journey."

A female doctor. She was young, too, and kind. Eleanor continued staring until she saw the woman was waiting for her to say something. "Mrs. Sullivan has been so nice to me. I was very tired. Still am really but I have plenty of time to rest. I don't have to go to meet the teachers at the school until the day after tomorrow."

"Laura and Ellen are lovely. I recommend a long soak in a bathtub. I can remember sitting on those hard train seats. I felt I would never get the feeling back in my lower regions," Erin had leaned in to whisper.

Shocked, Eleanor wasn't sure how to respond. The lady was a doctor but still it wasn't done to discuss anatomy in the street.

"Doc Erin, come quick. You're needed."

"I am so sorry, Miss Templeton. Duty calls. I can't wait to get to know you better."

She was gone before Eleanor could answer. She hoped the emergency would turn out to be a false alarm.

* * *

Worried sick, Erin ran to the orphanage after stopping at the clinic to grab her medical bag.

"Thank God you were in town. It's Wilma, she's collapsed. I don't know what's wrong with her."

"Please don't worry, Father Molloy. I don't want a second patient," she said trying to reassure him. "Wilma will be fine, she probably just over did it."

Erin examined Wilma, her heart was racing a little

too quickly but apart from that, she couldn't find anything wrong. She instructed the others to carry Wilma to her bedroom.

* * *

SOMETIME LATER, Wilma woke up. She was lying in bed but couldn't remember how she had got there. Someone had undressed her and put her into her nightgown. Her cheeks flamed. She remembered talking to Father Molloy. She'd been out of sorts with him. But then it was all a blur. She could hear someone coming. She closed her eyes again. She didn't have the energy to speak to anyone. She just wanted to sleep. She needed to get away from everyone and everything, even her dearest friends.

* * *

ERIN SAT by Wilma's bedside monitoring her breathing. She was sure the older woman had woken up but for some reason pretended to be still asleep. Erin didn't do anything. In her experience, a patient's body or mind often told them things but most people were too scared or sick to notice. Wilma's body had been screaming for a rest for a while now. Something had happened that pushed her over the edge. The best thing for her was rest and lots of it. As far as Erin was concerned Wilma needed to sleep and if pretending to be asleep helped her fall into a real sleep then so be it.

Ellen crept into the bedroom sometime later carrying a tray. "I didn't know if you wanted to eat here or go downstairs. If you would prefer to eat with the others, I will stay here with Wilma. I know you don't want her left alone."

"Ellen, do you know what upset Wilma today? Father Molloy said she was very cross and somewhat agitated."

Ellen shook her head but Erin sensed there was something.

"Ellen, please tell me, even if it seems silly. You live with Wilma, you know her better than I do."

"What do you think happened to her, Doc? Why did she pass out? Is she really ill?" Ellen wiped a tear from her eye. "I can't think what our lives would be like without her."

"Wilma isn't dying, Ellen." Erin sought to reassure the younger woman. "She is ill but not seriously enough to warrant what happened today. I think she is suffering from exhaustion."

"I knew she was doing too much. I tried to make her rest more but she was very cross. She accused me of wanting to get rid of her."

Erin looked at Wilma but this time she was genuinely asleep.

"Wilma is scared of growing old. Just like the rest of us. But she is particularly worried given the things she has seen in her lifetime. We talked about it some time back. I told her she had nothing to worry about. That her home would always be in Clover Springs."

"Of course it is. She is a huge part of Clover Springs. This town wouldn't be the same without her."

"So, Ellen, tell me about the last few days. What have you noticed? Has she been breathing with difficulty? Walking slower? Resting more? I want to know everything and anything you feel might be useful. The better picture I get the more I can help her."

"I haven't noticed her breathing, but she has been a bit slower on her feet than usual. I just assumed it was because you told her to rest more. But what is missing, is her smile and her laughter. She has such a wicked laugh. Once she starts the whole orphanage does. But the last few days that has been missing. She's still lovely to the children but she has been rather short with me on occasion. Samuel too. We just assumed she was annoyed with us for something, although that isn't like Wilma. She never holds grudges. She always says just what is on her mind."

"Go on, this is very helpful." Erin said quickly when Ellen stopped speaking, her face a mask of guilt.

"Ellen, I don't for a second believe you are doing anything other than telling me the truth. I found out a long time ago that a patient's mind is often responsible for their physical symptoms. I think in this case, although I can't be certain until I speak to Wilma, something is troubling her. She was so upset by whatever that is, she couldn't cope anymore. Her system basically said it needed to rest."

"Why couldn't she speak to us? Tell us what was wrong. We could have helped."

"Maybe, maybe not. I guess we will know more in time, but for now, we need to see she rests. I will speak to Mrs. Grey and Emer. I want someone to be here all the time round the clock until she recovers."

"I will do it."

"No, my friend, you won't. You have enough with Jake, the school, and the orphans. I will ask Lily to move in to help with the children until we leave for New York on the first. She is wonderful with Michelle."

CHAPTER 10

"Father Molloy, can you tell me what happened before Wilma collapsed?" Erin asked the old man softly. He was very upset. She could see how much he loved Wilma.

"It's all my fault. I put too much pressure on her. I always expected her to see the way out of my problems. I should have realized she wasn't feeling well."

"Why?"

"Why what, Doc?"

'Why would you think she wasn't feeling well? Did she tell you she had a headache or a pain in her chest?"

"No, but I knew she wasn't right. She was very cross for one thing. Wilma has a temper, I should know as I have been on the receiving end of it more than once but she is never unkind. She is always the first to help anyone. Yet today...she was different. She said she was tired. Too tired to help anyone else."

"That doesn't sound like Wilma, although I haven't known her as well as you have."

"It's not like her at all. Wilma would walk barefoot over stones to help someone. What's wrong with her, Doc? She isn't old. Well not to me," he said trying to smile but struggling.

Erin took his hand gently. "I believe Wilma is just exhausted both mentally and physically. We have no idea of what she experienced growing up, but I imagine she went through a lot. It takes someone who has known real pain to be able to help those who are going through heartache. She has taken on a lot. With Ellen being ill, the orphans, the worry of Laura, and all the rest of the comings and goings in the town she has had enough."

"So you don't think there is anything wrong with her physically?"

"I didn't say that. She is a big lady and her heart is under pressure. I've warned her before to rest more. But..."

"Doc, are you saying you think this is all in Wilma's mind?"

Erin sighed. If educated people like Father Molloy didn't believe her, what would her usual patients think.

"No, not all of it. I realize what I am about to say is believed to be mumbo jumbo by many doctors. But I have been doing a lot of reading about the brain and the mind and the impact on the body. I think Wilma is mentally exhausted in addition to being tired in the physical sense. I think her brain has decided she needs a rest. Basically, in very simple terms, her brain is protecting her body by making her take a rest." Erin looked at him wondering if she would see disbelief and mistrust, but instead, he seemed to be considering what she said.

"Little Beaver told me the Indians treat the whole person rather than just the symptoms of the illness. I believe there is a lot to their medicine, some of which we have yet to understand."

"Little Beaver and those of his people I have had the pleasure of meeting are very wise," Father Molloy commented.

"I think Wilma is hurting. I believe she needs someone to talk to. Someone she trusts who won't judge her. Someone like you, Father, but she needs to make the decision to talk."

"You think she is hiding a secret?"

"We all have secrets, Father," Erin said with a sad smile. "Now I must get back to my patient."

Erin walked back into Wilma's bedroom. She sensed the old woman was awake even though her eyes were closed.

"Dear Wilma, you have given us all quite a scare today. Yourself most of all. You need to rest. I insist. If I hear of you leaving this bed over the next two days, I will ask Mrs. Grey to watch you."

Wilma's eyes opened, her opinion of Mrs. Grey babysitting was clear to see from the look on her face. She didn't say a word though.

"Wilma, I know you are scared but you have no reason to be. You will be fine. Just do what I say. Okay?"

Erin waited until Wilma nodded in agreement. Then she leaned down and kissed the old woman on the cheek. "Please remember how much we all love you."

A tear trickled down Wilma's cheek. Erin brushed it away gently. "See you tomorrow."

Wilma didn't respond but turned her head to face the wall. Erin hoped she was correct in what she had told Father Molloy. Yes, she had been reading about the effects of past hurt and pain on people but it was in relation to soldiers' experiences at Antietam and other similarly bloody battles in the Civil War. As she looked at Wilma lying in the bed, her eyes closed, she didn't want to imagine the type of horrors this wonderful woman had experienced in her lifetime. Maybe it was time to call on Laura and find out what she knew of Wilma's background.

CHAPTER 11

Little Beaver accompanied Erin out to the Sullivan ranch. He didn't like any of the ladies traveling alone even though they had dealt with Dickinson and his gang.

"You think Wilma get better?"

"Yes, Little Beaver, I do. I think her heart is broken. But I do not know why."

"Much sadness in Wilma's face. She is kind and good and smiles at people but her eyes show much pain. Like many of our old people who live on reservations."

Erin wasn't sure what to say. She couldn't bear the thoughts of anyone living in such dire straits as the Indians were but there was nothing they could do about it. Apart from ensure the Indian community from Clover Springs remained safe.

"How is your wife and baby?"

"I tell you big secret?"

"Oh, please do. You know I won't tell anyone."

"My wife is having baby. I will have new child"

"Oh, Little Beaver, that is wonderful news. Please tell Asha I can come see her if she wishes. When I come back from New York."

"You like go big city? Me think it must be hard to breath with all the buildings and people."

Erin smiled at his screwed-up face. Sometimes his reactions reminded her of a young child. She turned to look at the Sullivan ranch as it came into view. She loved the house Mary's husband, Davy, had fashioned for her. He had built onto the old house his parents had lived in. Mary was a lucky woman with these magnificent views. She would love to live somewhere like that but it was too far from town to be practical for a doctor.

* * *

Mrs. Higgins was waiting for them when they drove up.

"I saw you coming over the hill. Good afternoon, Doc Erin, it's not often you come out visiting this way.

"You keep everyone so healthy with your cooking, I don't need to, Mrs. Higgins. Your skills are legendary."

"What's that husband of yours been telling you? He is a charmer that's for sure. Come in and have a drink. Mary would love to chat. She could talk all day Miss Mary, and I don't have time to be listening." Mrs. H smiled showing Erin she loved Miss Mary dearly. "Little Beaver would you like a drink or do you want to find Davy?"

"I go find Davy before Miss Mary sees me. She talk a lot!" Little Beaver ran leaving the two amused women behind him.

"I actually need to see Laura for a few minutes. Maybe she will come back with me and we could all have some coffee?" Erin asked.

"Perfect, Doc. You take your time."

Erin wondered if she might be able to find out about Mrs. H and Cookie while she was here. But first she had to speak to Laura. She drove the wagon down to Laura's house which was situated on the property next to the ranch.

"Good afternoon, Mrs. Kelley, could I please come in?" Erin knocked on Laura's door.

"Please do, Doc Erin. And call me Laura. Every time someone says Mrs. Kelley, my heart goes to my mouth. I look for my mother-in-law."

Erin smiled. She had met the infamous Mrs. Kelley and couldn't blame Laura for wanting to avoid her. From what she had heard, Laura's husband Paul was so different to his mother some folks believed him to be adopted.

"What can I do for you, Doc? I mean I love the fact you've called but you are here for something other than a chat, aren't you?"

"Are you always this direct, Laura?"

"No, I used to be a lot worse." Laura smiled.

"I am here about Wilma. She is fine but you should know she collapsed yesterday."

Panic filled Laura's eyes. "Wilma? She couldn't. What's wrong with her? Did she catch something from the children? Are they sick too?"

"Please calm down, Laura. From what Mrs. Grey has told me about your own heart condition, you shouldn't get too excited. Wilma will be fine. You can come back into town with me to visit her if you like. I called to see if you could tell me anything that will help me to find a way to make her better.

"What do you mean? I don't know much about doctoring."

"I didn't mean in that way. Why don't you sit down? I believe Wilma is exhausted. I have asked her to slow down. She does more work than most women in their early twenties. So there is a physical reason for why she collapsed. She needs to rest more and lose some weight."

"Yes, I have been telling her that for ages. She takes

on way too much. But then when I was sick she minded my baby."

"And she loved doing it. She sees your baby as her grandchild. That is partly why I came to speak to you in private. How much do you know of Wilma's past?"

A guarded look came over Laura's face. Erin hastened to reassure her.

"I am not asking out of nosiness. From some of the things Wilma has said recently, to me and to Father Molloy and others, I believe she is running from something. Not physically running but there is something disturbing her sleep. Maybe memories of some past issue. I need to know as much as possible about her in order to help. I will not repeat it to anyone. I promise."

Laura sat in silence, her eyes glued to Erin as if weighing up whether she could trust her or not.

"Laura, if it helps, I heard the gossip about how you came to Clover Springs. About Coleman and the others. I don't judge anyone. I am sure you heard about me."

"I heard you wanted to kill your husband." Laura spoke softly. "Not Mick, the other one."

Although she hated talking about Anthony, her first husband, now was the time for honesty. "Yes, I did."

"I did too. I think I would have if it weren't for

Wilma," Laura said quietly. "I know I would have died if she hadn't saved me. I owe her everything."

"Tell me how you got to know her."

Erin listened as Laura told her about her past life before she came to Clover Springs. In a way, some of her story reminded her of Mollie only Laura had been older and had actually married her abuser. Laura described Wilma as a sort of guardian angel doing what she did best. Protecting the girls as much as she could from the abusive life they lived.

"So you believe Wilma worked in one of these houses too?"

It took Laura a long time to answer.

"I don't know for certain. We never discussed it. But I knew she had been there a long time. She understood what the other girls were going through. She was tough on them, they complained to the police after my husband was killed. They said she was abusive. But she wasn't. She was trying to protect them by not allowing them to drink themselves to death. I did wonder but who knows? She certainly had been in my husband's service for some number of years."

"Did she ever speak to you about her days as a slave?"

Laura shook her head but Erin believed she was holding something back.

"Nothing at all?"

"Just this one time. I'd been beaten very badly. I thought I was going to die. I wanted to. But Wilma refused to let me. She told me to fight back. Someone could own your body but nobody but you owned your soul. I screamed at her. I asked her what would she know about it? And then she showed me."

Laura couldn't go on. Erin let her cry and then gave her time to compose herself.

"I never saw anything like those marks. She didn't tell me why she had them. She never showed them to me again."

Erin suspected the marks were on Wilma's back. She had never seen the woman undressed.

"Do you think her time as a slave is affecting her now?" Laura's eyes were full of disbelief.

"I don't know, Laura, but she said she wasn't sleeping. She told Father Molloy it was the new pills I gave her but they should be helping her to sleep. She said she had bad dreams. I know I often dreamed of Anthony in those first weeks after he died. I was sure he was coming back for me."

"I did too. Maybe Wilma is worried someone from her past will come for her. Slavery is gone now, they wouldn't be able to take her away."

"Yes, but sometimes our minds don't always see the

truth." Erin stood up. "I promised Mrs. Higgins I would call in for coffee. Will you join us?"

"I will in a while. I just want to get a meal ready for Paul. Please don't go back to Clover Springs without me. I want to check on Wilma for myself. She's been like a mother to me for a long time now. I couldn't bear if anything were to happen to her."

Erin wondered if Wilma had any idea how many people believed she had saved their lives. She doubted the older woman knew just how highly people thought of her.

SHE HEADED BACK to the Sullivan ranch where she had an enjoyable visit with Mary and Mrs. Higgins. She told the two ladies about Wilma and both expressed their concern for the patient. Little Beaver put his head around the door to say he was off. He would ride one of Davy's horses back to town. Once Laura arrived, Erin drove them both back to Clover Springs laden with pies and other things, including a book. Mary thought Wilma might like to read it while she was resting. She should really check on the new teacher but that visit would have to wait until another day.

CHAPTER 12

Laura's visit with Wilma didn't go very well. It was obvious she had been crying when Erin spoke to her.

"She didn't talk to me. Barely one sentence in that whole time. I talked about everything I could think of. The baby, Paul, and even my mother-in-law. Speaking about Mrs. Kelley is usually enough to get Wilma all fired up but she didn't even remark on it today. You said she was going to get better. When?"

Erin knew Laura wasn't really angry with her but frustrated with the fact her friend, no, her family member was ill.

"Wilma hasn't been ill for long, Laura, you have to be patient. She will be the same as usual in a couple of weeks or so."

"Do you really believe that?"

"Yes, Laura, I do," Erin said without adding provided we get some luck and a lot of prayers. Laura followed Erin downstairs. Lily had said she would sit with Wilma for a while.

* * *

Father Molloy was waiting in the kitchen. He knew there was no change in Wilma but he wanted to speak to Laura and Ellen about the new school teacher.

"Ladies, I have some good news to put a little smile back on those faces. I found a new school teacher. Her name is Miss Templeton and she comes highly recommended."

"Oh, that is wonderful, Father Molloy. Wilma will..." Ellen's voice trailed off.

"Wilma will be delighted just as soon as she knows." Erin said firmly. "Now tell us more about Miss Templeton, Father, where is she from? What brings her to Clover Springs? What age is she?"

"Erin, are you sure you are not Mary Sullivan in disguise? I never thought anyone could ask as many questions as quick as Mary but you now hold the record," Father Molloy said, his eyes telling her he knew what she was doing and approved.

Everyone laughed at the teasing and for a couple of

minutes the kitchen was just like it was when Wilma was present.

"I am not sure what age Miss Templeton is, I would guess about your age Ellen. She travelled here from Britain. She recently lost her father, his death having a negative impact on her family situation. She studied at Cheltenham Ladies College so is well educated. She seems to be of good character and moral standing too. I like her although she is quiet and rather shy."

"She won't stay that way for long. Not with us two chatting to her all day long." Ellen said smiling at Laura. "Wonder how long it will be before she gets married?"

"Married? She has only just arrived," Erin replied.

"Yes, but if she is as lovely as she sounds, she won't stay single for long. Not around here," Ellen said firmly.

Erin caught a look of sadness in Father Molloy's eyes. Wilma wasn't the only one keeping secrets. Neither Laura nor Ellen seemed to notice so Erin kept her thoughts to herself.

"I best be getting home or my husband will be out looking for a new wife," Erin joked as she stood up. She was dying for a hug from Mick and a kiss from Michelle. After such a long and trying day, she was thrilled she had a family of her own to go home to. She was lucky.

* * *

MICK WAS WAITING for her when she got home. He gave her a hug, holding her close as she struggled to maintain her composure. Seeing Wilma laid low had taken more of a toll on her than she'd realized. Mick wrapped his arm around her waist as he escorted her in to see their daughter. Michelle was thriving. She was sleeping with her thumb in her mouth.

"She's just gorgeous, isn't she?" Erin whispered.

"She is when she is asleep. She wasn't too happy earlier I can tell you." Mick pouted. "I think she prefers when her ma is here to put her to bed."

"Well, if today is anything to go by, she best get used to her pa. I am exhausted."

"I got your bath ready. You just go and relax. Dinner is ready whenever you want to eat."

"I don't know why I got so lucky. But I am glad you married me."

"I am too, darlin', more than I can ever say." He proceeded to kiss her showing her how much he cared. Soon the bath was the last thing on either of their minds.

* * *

Sometime later, Mick cradled Erin in his arms. "What's wrong, darling?"

"I don't know if I should go to New York. Don't be mad."

He sat up in the bed, looking at her. "I won't be angry but why? I thought you really wanted to go."

"I do. I get the feeling something is wrong with Mrs. Doherty. She was good to me and I want to make sure she is all right. But Wilma needs me here."

"But you said Wilma's troubles weren't of a medical nature, at least not that you could cure."

"Yes, but she's my friend and what if I am wrong? What if it is something medical and if I am in New York..."

"Doc will deal with it just as he did when you were away studying. Mrs. Grey is here and Emer Shipley. You are a wonderful doctor but even you need a vacation."

Erin smiled a wickedly beautiful smile. "It's our honeymoon."

"Yes, me darling, it is. Personally, I think I am worth spending time with."

"Well, if you continue to kiss me like that, maybe I could agree."

He tickled her as she burst into giggles. "I love Doc Erin but it would be nice to spend time with Erin Quinn for a little bit."

"Mmmm."

"We can be a real family—just you, me and Michelle."

"What about Lily? She's been helping out at the orphanage."

"Someone else can do that. Lily is coming with us. I am not leaving her here with Ma Kelley and her cronies on the warpath."

Erin pulled him closer to her and kissed him. "I love your big heart, Mick Quinn. Come here and let me show you how much."

CHAPTER 13

Gary couldn't get the picture of the new teacher out of his head. There was something really sad and suspicious about her being in Clover Springs. She walked and talked like a real lady and had the fancy clothes, but what would her type be doing teaching school in Clover Springs of all places? He could see her working as a governess, but even then, she would be a bit overdressed.

He wanted to ask Father Molloy but the priest hadn't been near the saloon since the new teacher arrived. If Doc Erin was not busy with tending Wilma and packing for New York, she would have invited the teacher to dinner. He polished some glasses before replacing them on the shelf.

"Did you hear one of your people arrived in town?"

"My people, Murph? I wasn't aware of any family members visiting Clover Springs."

"Not a relation. But she's British." Murph's face looked like he had just bitten into something rotten.

"How do you know?"

"Someone told me she went to college in Cheltenham. That's in England. They used to have some fine horse racing there until some guy bought the land and stopped it. He hated horses. Imagine a British man hating horse racing."

Gary worked away, only half listening to Murph who could talk the back legs off a donkey. "Anyway, I know it's in Britain. She sounds British too."

"You've spoken to her?"

Murph turned red. "Not really. I was behind her in the queue in the store. Katie Sullivan took so long talking to her I forgot what I went in to buy."

Gary smiled. Murph would forget his own head if it wasn't attached to his neck. "I hope you won't hold the fact she is British against her. She has come to teach the children. Father Molloy says she is highly qualified."

"Did he? And he an Irishman!"

"Murph, since when did your nationality determine whether you were good or bad at something? Give her a chance, will you?"

Murph muttered into his drink. Gary didn't listen

as he'd heard enough. Although he'd told Father Molloy that Murph didn't mean it, his constant harping on about all English people being a curse on society got a bit wearing at times.

"Wonder how long she'll last?"

"In Clover Springs? I imagine a while as the school keeps expanding."

"No, dummy. As a single woman. She's quite a looker if you go for the dark eyes and hair. Prefer a blonde myself." Murph burped loudly before draining his glass.

Gary busied himself cleaning another shelf. He didn't want to think about the pretty school teacher.

* * *

He didn't get much of a chance to stop thinking about Miss Templeton as the whole town was talking about her. He had only come out to the store for some flour and other store items and a group of men were outside, talking.

"I heard her father was a duke, that would make her a real lady." Charlie Staunton pushed out his chest. "I am going to ask her to the dance. She will be used to real gentlemen."

"Won't have much interest in you then, will she?" Daniel Sullivan joked making the other men laugh.

"You take that back. You are only a thick Irish paddy who wouldn't recognize a gentleman if he stood in front of you."

"Watch it, Staunton, or you won't be doing any standing anywhere. Nobody insults my pa and gets away with it. Yes, he was Irish but unlike some around here, he didn't lack intelligence or manners." Daniel's reply made Staunton's cheeks redden but he stayed quiet. Daniel was known to be mild mannered until it came to his family. Then he would fight tougher than the rest of them.

"What's the daughter of an English lord doing in Clover Springs? She could have gone to New York. Isn't that where the rich live?" a friend of Staunton's asked.

"Seems suspicious to me. Why would any member of a rich and titled family be working as a teacher? I reckon she just made the whole thing up."

"That's enough. Nobody knows Miss Templeton's background, but she is new to our town and deserves some respect and courtesy." Gary surprised himself most of all by speaking out. Usually, he kept his opinions to himself.

"You would say that given she is one of yours."

Gary glared at the cowboy. "If in that pea-sized brain of yours you think the fact she appears to be British means she warrants better treatment, you are mistaken. Every lady, be they nobly born or not, deserves a man's courtesy and respect. Didn't your mother teach you anything?"

"I never knew my ma."

* * *

GARY TURNED his back on the conversation just in time to see Miss Templeton walking away, her cheeks crimson. She must have heard the conversation or at least part of it. He walked faster to catch up with her.

"My apologies, Miss Templeton. The men didn't mean any harm."

She gave him a dirty look but didn't say a word.

"I am sorry. You weren't supposed to hear them." Why was he apologizing? He hadn't said anything.

"You mean you would have continued to gossip about my person in private. I expected such behavior from a bunch of old women but…" She stopped talking. He suspected she was too emotional to finish her sentence.

He twirled his hat in his hands for a couple of seconds. "I am sincerely sorry you heard any of it. Clover Springs is a small place and the arrival of any new face, especially if I may be so bold as to say a young, attractive lady, will be the subject of conversation."

She glanced back at the group of men. "Should I give them the real facts of my life to date?"

"I wouldn't. What they will make up will be far more interesting," he joked, hoping to make her smile but it didn't. "What I mean is you should not have to explain yourself to anyone."

"Thank you, mister…"

"Gary Barrett, ma'am." He made a half bow as he introduced himself.

"Thank you, Mr. Barrett. I believe you are trying to be kind."

The look on her face plainly said she thought he was failing but before he could say anything else, he was dismissed with a rather cold tone.

"Good day."

He stood looking after her as she continued her journey down the street.

"Good morning, Gary. I see you met our new teacher. She will be a wonderful addition to Clover Springs."

"Yes, Father, if she stays."

The older man looked perplexed. "She has only just arrived. Is she thinking of leaving already?"

"Seems she may have overhead some unfortunate gossip this morning."

Father Molloy's eyes darkened. "What type of

gossip? Why would anyone want to talk about a respectable young lady?"

"Because she is young and pretty. The men have set their sights on her. Charlie Staunton seems to think she is the daughter of an English duke."

The look in Father Molloys' eyes suggested Charlie might have been closer to the truth than anyone realized.

"Her history and background doesn't matter. Why can't people keep their opinions to themselves? The world would be a much easier place if everyone kept a vow of silence."

Gary was left staring at the priest as he marched away. It was so unlike Father Molloy. There was something more to this than a few men making comments. Father Molloy knew as well as anyone the arrival of a young, single lady to Clover Springs was bound to generate interest. She'd be lucky if she survived a week before being inundated with marriage proposals.

He wished Doc Erin was here to speak to the new schoolteacher but she had driven out to see Mrs. Grey. He wished there was another woman he felt comfortable asking for help but there wasn't.

CHAPTER 14

Erin pulled up outside Mrs. Grey's home. She hoped her friend would understand her taking time off to go to New York. She jumped down from the wagon, tied the horse to the rail, and knocked on the front door. It was opened promptly by Mrs. Grey dressed to go out.

"Mrs. Grey, are you busy?"

"Come in, Doc. I heard a wagon drive up but wasn't expecting you to be driving. I thought you favored riding."

"I do but I was hoping I would be able to give you a lift into town," Erin said, trying not to alarm Mrs. Grey.

"That is very nice of you. I was just on my way to the clinic. Is something wrong? It is, isn't it?" Mrs. Grey asked, her voice rising slightly with worry.

"I need your help. Have you heard about Wilma?" Erin asked softly.

"No, what happened?"

"She collapsed at the orphanage. I think..." Before Erin could elaborate, Mrs. Grey interrupted.

"Her heart?"

"I don't think it helped but I think it's more than that. She has been lying down for three days," Erin said, wondering how she could say that she thought it was more of a mental issue than a physical one.

"Why didn't you come get me before?"

"We expected Wilma to recover."

"But she hasn't?"

"Physically she has. Her breathing is back to normal and the rest in bed has done her heart some good. But... I don't know and I feel a little silly even saying it out loud, but I think Wilma has decided she has had enough."

"Enough of what?" Mrs. Grey's curious stare made Erin feel even more uncomfortable. What if she was wrong and Wilma had something seriously wrong with her? But she had grown used to listening to the voice in her head.

"Mrs. Grey, I honestly don't know. I just have a feeling. Wilma has been acting differently for a little while now. I thought she was tired so I gave her something to help her sleep."

"Did she take too much?" Mrs. Grey demanded. Anyone watching them would think she was cross, but Erin knew her well enough to know the gruff exterior hid a heart of gold.

"No, in fact, she doesn't seem to have taken any of the medicine I gave her. The bottle looks as full as it was leaving the clinic." Erin looked at the other woman. "I know you have experience of nursing during the war. I have been doing some reading on the soldiers who just gave up. Those that were expected to recover and didn't."

"Wilma isn't in a war!"

The dubious expression on the other woman's face as well as her stating the obvious nearly made Erin give up. But instead, she decided to just say it. "I have been reading about soldiers who suffer relapse some years later. Mick still has nightmares, although I don't think he would be happy with my sharing that information. I wonder if some trauma Wilma went through is now eating her up inside."

Mrs. Grey remained silent. Erin waited, not sure if she should give the woman a moment to think or if she should say something else. But what? If she was wrong, the people of Clover Springs would think she had lost her mind.

"What would you like me to do, Doc?"

"You are Wilma's friend."

"She has closer friends."

Erin got the impression Mrs. Grey was trying to avoid seeing Wilma but she didn't understand why.

"She has young friends like Laura, Ellen, Alicia, and even me. But you are nearer in age to Wilma. You may have some insight into what she is dealing with."

Mrs. Grey paced making Erin feel even more uncomfortable. Had she made a big mistake coming here?

"Mrs. Grey, I came for three reasons. One, because I think you and Wilma are closer friends than you are leading me to believe. I know she admires and respects you and you feel the same way for her. But even more importantly, I have seen you in action and heard stories about your deeds. You are not a quitter. You have a strength of character few can mirror."

"I am not the right person for Wilma to speak to. Can't you ask Father Molloy?"

"It's a female friend she needs."

"Has she said that?"

"No, she hasn't said anything," Erin admitted reluctantly.

Mrs. Grey stopped pacing and sat down. "Erin, what do you know about me?"

"Enough to know you are a wonderful nurse and a good friend."

"I was born on a plantation outside Richmond. My

father owned slaves. Our family used people like Wilma to attend to their every need. When my father needed more male slaves, he sold the female ones. He broke up families and sent them to the auction block where they likely as not never saw their mothers or children again," Mrs. Grey blurted out, her hands shanking with agitation.

"You didn't do that, Mrs. Grey," Erin spoke softly trying to hide her shock. Of course she knew Mrs. Grey originally came from the south as she still had the accent, particularly when someone annoyed her. But she hadn't given the issue of owning slaves any further thought.

"No, but I was part of the society who kept amazing people like Wilma tethered like animals. Worse than livestock."

"Does Wilma know about your past?"

"I don't know. It isn't something we discussed."

"Well, maybe now is a good time to start. She may just get so fired up at the story you tell, she will come back to us fighting." Erin smiled but Mrs. Grey didn't smile back. "Mrs. Grey, you weren't responsible for what your father or your society did but now you have a real chance to help. Can't you try? Wilma would help you if the situation was reversed."

"Yes, she would. I will try, Doc, but you mark my

words, this could be the biggest mistake we have ever made."

"It could also be the best decision. I will ask Father Molloy to pray for us."

Mrs. Grey stood up. "Let me get my shawl and my bible. I can read a little for Wilma."

As they rode back into town, Mrs. Grey asked. "Erin, you said there was a third reason for asking me."

"There is and I feel rather guilty about it, especially given how long I was away studying."

"But…" Mrs. Grey prompted.

"Alicia and her family are going to New York. They offered to bring us as well, as a wedding present. I have friends in the city whom I would love to see. My old housekeeper Mrs. Doherty has written to me, but her letter isn't as upbeat as she would normally be. I fear she may have suffered financially due to the scandal surrounding me."

"Oh, you poor girl. You can't be blamed for any of that. Of course you must go. As you said, you can't do any more for Wilma, and Doc is here if we need him."

"But what if I am wrong?"

"About Wilma? I doubt that very much. I haven't worked with you for long but I think you are an excellent doctor. You think not only with your head but with your heart. You have an instinct for your patients. It's a good thing."

"So you don't mind?" Erin asked.

"I will miss you. We all will. But you are a newly married woman. It's time to make a fuss of your husband and he of you. You and Mick share something beautiful. Don't ever let it die or come second to anything or anyone else. Promise me?"

Feeling rather overcome by the sincerity behind Mrs. Grey's words, Erin nodded as she couldn't speak. She thanked the Lord for the day she had landed in Clover Springs.

"I will look after Wilma. Don't worry about her. Just come back safely. We don't want to lose you to New York. You belong here."

Erin wanted to hug the older woman but felt it might be inappropriate, so instead, squeezed her arm. "Thank you," she whispered.

CHAPTER 15

Doc Erin dropped Mrs. Grey off at the orphanage but didn't come in with her. She had to go back to the clinic to make sure there weren't any last-minute emergencies to deal with before she left for New York.

Mrs. Grey stood outside the door of the orphanage for so long Samuel opened it and asked her if she was coming in or not. She knew he was teasing but she couldn't smile. She was too worried about Wilma.

"Mrs. Grey, please don't look so concerned. Wilma will get better. She will be very pleased you are here." Samuel had spoken kindly as he held the door open and offered her his good hand to help her inside. She took it as her legs felt shaky.

"Would you like some coffee here or will I send it up to you later?"

"I don't need coffee but thank you, Samuel, for your kindness," she said in a shaky voice.

* * *

Mrs. Grey pushed the bedroom door open quietly not wanting to wake Wilma if she was asleep. Part of her hoped she was. She loved Wilma, but would her speaking about her past ruin their friendship? Until now, they had always worked off the basis the past should be left in the past. But was that just the coward's way out?

She moved toward the bed. Wilma was awake but instead of her usual cheery greeting, she remained silent.

"Good morning, Wilma, bit late for you to still be in bed, isn't it?" Mrs. Grey teased but when there was no response from Wilma she changed her tone. "Wilma whatever your surname is, don't you close your eyes to me. You got to get over this...whatever this is. We need you up. Clover Springs isn't the same without you."

Wilma still didn't react, making Mrs. Grey extremely worried.

She sat at the edge of the bed taking one of Wilma's hands. "Come on, Wilma, speak to me. Tell me what is wrong."

Her friend's big brown eyes focused on her but she got the impression she wasn't seeing her but something else. It sent a shiver down her spine. "Talk to me, please. Don't tell anyone but you are scaring me."

That last comment generated half a smile before Wilma returned to staring at a spot somewhere above Mrs. Grey's head.

"Wilma, can't you tell me? You know I would never hold anything against you. It doesn't matter what it is."

"I have a daughter. Or at least I had," Wilma whispered, a lone tear making its way down her cheek. "I thought I saw her the other day, walking toward the school house, but it couldn't be her. She was too young for a start. Just something about the way she walked reminded me of my Solace."

"Your daughter? Here in Clover Springs?" Mrs. Grey tried to hide her shock. Wilma had never mentioned a child before.

"Not my daughter. Solace is dead. It's all my fault."

Wilma started sobbing. Not genteel ladylike sobs but heart rendering sobs that threatened to tear her body apart. Mrs. Grey lost hold of her hand and put her arms around her pulling her close. "Cry, Wilma, let the hurt out. Then you can tell me all about Solace."

Wilma cried for ages but Mrs. Grey didn't say a word as she knew her friend had to let her feelings go. She had spent far too long locking them inside. With a last heaving sigh, she pushed Mrs. Grey gently away. Mrs. Grey gave her a hanky.

"Tell me about Solace. When did you last see her?"

"Eighteen sixty-four. The master of the house was away fighting. The Union Army came. They were supposed to be our saviors but they didn't act like it. The soldiers, they was bored. They came to the slaves' quarters and started whipping some of the field hands. Not 'cause they did anything but just 'cause they had nothin' better to do. I begged Solace to hide but she never could stand by when there was any form of injustice. She didn't listen to me. She grabbed one of the whips and struck the leader of the group. Hard. I grabbed her and tole her to run. I took the whip and started fighting those soldiers back. A few of the other slaves turned on them too. She and Andrew, her best friend, they both took off and ran for all they was worth. I ain't never seen them again."

"Wilma, you didn't kill her. You gave her her freedom. It sounds like those white boys were only out for mischief anyway."

Wilma fell quiet. She went back to staring at the wall again.

"Wilma, what happened next?"

"The soldiers' leader, he was a captain, he came when they started firing their guns. He wanted to know what was wrong. The soldiers told him a pack of lies about how we was making trouble and they were just tryin' to teach us a lesson. He didn't believe them though. At least he didn't seem to. He tole me I had to go with him to the master's house. I went. I didn't wait behind for my little girl to be found."

"Wilma, you didn't have a choice. The soldiers would have forced you to obey the captain."

"Maybe, but we will never knows that. Anyway, he take me up to the big house. I shouldn't have been in the slaves' quarters anyway. House slaves weren't supposed to go down there without permission but something tole me my girl needed me. Anyway, he made me go upstairs and get dressed into one of the mistress' gowns. I was shakin' so bad as we was never allowed to touch her dresses. Only her maid was allowed to do that. Then he insisted I sit down and eat a meal with him. It was horrible. He was pretending he was the master and I the mistress. He said he could just imagine the plantation owner's grief knowing we was using his best service and eating at his table with a slave dressed in his wife's clothes.

"What happened then?" Mrs. Grey asked quietly.

"He gave me a choice. Well, he tole me it was a choice. He said if I came willingly with him, he would order his men not to look for the escaped slaves. If I didn't go, he would kill one slave for every minute the slaves were missing."

Mrs. Grey waited for Wilma to speak.

"I guess you don't understand what it was like. I had to go. I couldn't let them kill my people."

"Of course you had to go, Wilma. Did he mean to give you your freedom?"

"Freedom? What white man ever really wanted to free a slave?" Wilma sneered. It was so unlike her, Mrs. Grey was shocked.

"My David did. He worked with the Underground Railway. He saved many slaves who ran to Canada."

"How did you know? Did he tole you? He could have just been saying stuff."

"I helped him," Mrs. Grey whispered.

Distrust and fear caused Wilma's eyes to open wider. She went to take her hand away but Mrs. Grey held onto it tightly.

"Wilma, my father owned a plantation just like the one you lived on. He had lots of slaves. I used to teach them how to read and write. My father was a decent owner."

"Ain't no such thing."

"Well no, not from your perspective but in terms of what other plantation owners did, he was a good master. He gave his people plenty of food and shelter."

"Did he give them their freedom?"

Mrs. Grey shook her head.

"Did he keep families together?"

"No, Wilma, he didn't. That's why I helped David."

"You helped your father's slaves to escape? Why you done that?"

"I believed it was wrong to keep people enslaved like animals. I believed then and believe today all people are equal. The color of your skin doesn't make you who you are."

"But you still lived on the plantation, or did you run away with your friend?"

"No, I stayed and it is something I will regret as long as I live. If I had ran, I could have married David years earlier than I did. We might have had a family, and we would have had more time together."

"I can't believe you never tole me you was a plantation owner."

"I was never that, Wilma."

"I tole you my story and the whole time you was laughing at me. What did you think of me? I guess I am just a stupid black ne—"

"Don't you dare ever use that word to describe anyone let along yourself. Now you can lie on that bed feeling sorry for yourself or you can get your big backside out of it. You tell me you lost your daughter. What have you done about finding her?"

Wilma turned to stare at the wall.

"You haven't tried to find her, not after all these years? Why?"

"I left without knowing whether she was alive or dead. What if she came back to find me and I wasn't there? I should have stayed."

"Wilma, you couldn't stay, you would have been killed just like the rest of the slaves. By going, you potentially saved her life, but you definitely saved the lives of the rest of the slaves on the plantation. If they survived the war, they would have been freed."

Wilma didn't respond.

"Did you ever try to get back to the plantation to check?"

"I wasn't able to leave."

"But you weren't his slave."

"Not by law but he tole me he'd kill me. He'd track me down and nobody would care as I was only an ole…"

"Oh, Wilma, what horrors you have been through. And yet you always are there to help someone else."

"I used to pretend that if I helped people maybe someone would help my little girl. But it's stupid, ain't it? We just got to look at Rosa and John to see nobody wants those that don't fit in."

"Solace was part white?"

Wilma nodded.

"Maybe she did survive. She might be living somewhere with her own family."

"I was tole she was dead."

"By who?"

"Laura's husband. He said he'd tracked her down but she died of disease. A bad one."

"And you believed him?"

"I didn't have any reason not to."

"You had plenty of reason. You saw the way he treated those girls in his house. The way he treated Laura. I'm guessing your captain didn't treat you as kindly as you implied in the story. What happened to him anyway, did he survive the war?"

Wilma nodded.

"Where did you end up?"

"Boston."

"So how did you meet Laura's husband? She said you worked for him for a long time."

"He was the captain's son."

CHAPTER 16

Gary walked toward the boarding house wondering how he should phrase his apology and request. Every time he thought of Miss Templeton, he saw her wide brown eyes filled with tears and her stricken face as she stood listening to the men gossiping about her. He wished for the thousandth time he hadn't decided to go to the store. He could have waited till later in the day.

Should he ask Mrs. Sullivan to formerly introduce them and then apologize? He'd been reading some books set in England, and they seemed very set on correct manners. He couldn't remember enough of his time in London, and it wasn't as if they rubbed shoulders with the type of people Miss Templeton was used to.

He didn't notice her sitting on the porch, a shawl wrapped around her legs, until he was practically standing beside her. She was holding a book, although she didn't seem to be reading it.

"Good afternoon, Mr. Barrett. How can I help you?"

Gary stood gazing at her, his tongue getting so twisted he couldn't form a sentence. He swallowed hard but still nothing.

She closed the book to stare at him, probably wondering if he had been struck dumb.

"Yes?"

"Miss Templeton, I just wanted to apologize for what you heard outside the store. I am sure you aren't used to people gossiping about you. I don't think anyone meant any harm, only beautiful, single women are rare in Clover Springs and…"

"Please don't apologize again. You already did that at the store. I should be the one apologizing. I was upset. I appreciate the fact you told them all women should be treated with respect."

He smiled at her. "Mum told me over and over again to make sure I never forgot. I am glad you don't hold a grudge." He stood there staring at her, trying to get the confidence to ask her.

"Was there something else?"

"Miss Templeton, I was wondering…em what I

mean to ask…do you have an escort for the Easter dance?" Easter? It was only February. She was going to think he was an idiot. "I know it's early, the dance was supposed to be this weekend but it was postponed due to Doc Erin and the others going to New York." He was talking too much.

"No, I don't," she said, "but I won't be going so it is of no matter."

"Why?"

"I don't have to answer to you, Mr. Barrett."

"No, you don't, of course not. I just wondered why you wouldn't be going. It's a great way to get to know people from the community."

"I teach the children. They are the only people I am interested in getting to know any better."

"Well, of all the high and mighty attitudes I have come across, yours takes the biscuit. What is wrong with you? Are we not good enough to associate with the daughter of a lord or earl or whatever title your father holds?"

She laughed, a harsh rather than pleasant sound, but it was the tears in her eyes that cut him to the core.

"Gossip sure flies fast around this town. I don't know what you have been told, Mr. Barrett, but I am not the daughter of a title. Nor am I in anyway snobbish. I just happen to have learned quite recently it is better not to open yourself up to more heartbreak. Making friends leaves one vulnerable."

She stood up and walked away without a single backward glance. He had been well and truly dismissed, not to mention put in his place and he thoroughly deserved it. What sort of idiot was he to mention gossip to a lady? He'd accused Murph of judging her when he had done the exact same thing. He'd hurt her, too, which was unforgiveable.

* * *

WHY DID she always get flustered whenever he was around? If her nanny could see her now, she would be on bread and water for a week. Young ladies were brought up to be pleasant. Not warm necessarily but always polite. She had been nearly rude. All he had done was ask her to accompany him to a dance.

"Would you like some coffee, Miss Templeton, I just made a fresh pot. Oh, are you all right, dear, you look rather flushed."

"I am fine, thank you. I think I may have sat out a little too long. Its colder than I thought."

Mrs. Sullivan looked at her, disbelief written all over her face but at least she didn't pry.

"I heard there is an Easter dance. Do you always celebrate Easter like that?" she asked.

"No, not usually. Father Molloy hoped to have it this weekend but he had to postpone it. Good job too really. A couple of years back, the Orphanage, or Hope House to give it it's proper name, was built. But as you can see from school, we have a lot of orphans. They need more space but as usual there is a shortage of funds. Wilma and Father Molloy thought we could do something similar to a barn raising. Do they have them in England?"

Eleanor shook her head.

"It's where the community gets together to build a house or a barn. The men, there are enough of them, can get a building up in a day. The dance in the evening is a reward where they can share some fine food and dancing."

"Where will it be held?"

"Well, to be honest, I don't think they have thought it through properly. In the summer a barn raising, is held outdoors. The weather is warm and sunny. Hopefully, Easter will be warm. There isn't anywhere big enough in town to hold it indoors."

"What type of dances do they do?" Eleanor couldn't resist asking. She'd loved parties back home. Her dancing was one of the few things her grandmother ever complimented her on.

"Irish reels and some set dances and maybe the odd waltz. Not the type of dances you would be used to, I imagine. But it's good fun to learn the new steps. If you have time, I can teach you a couple."

Although tempted, Eleanor refused. She had just told Mr. Barrett she wasn't going dancing. She was a woman of her word.

CHAPTER 17

Erin was the last on the platform. She was still torn about going to New York.

"Get on the train, Doc, your family is waiting," Mrs. Grey said kindly.

"I will send a telegram as soon as we arrive. It will have my contact details. If you need me, send for me."

"Erin, will you please go. I am going to take Wilma away for a few days. A change of scene will do her good."

Erin frowned. "Where are you going? Who will look after the clinic?" she asked. "Oh, that sounded selfish. I didn't mean it like that."

"Erin Quinn, we survived before you arrived in Clover Springs. We will be fine for two weeks. Doc and Emer Shipley can cope. Now please get on the train before it leaves without you."

"Thank you, Mrs. Grey. I am being silly."

"Not silly, just too caring about everyone but yourself. Please have a good time and don't worry about Wilma. She will be fine."

"Goodbye."

Mrs. Grey stood on the platform waving as the train pulled out of the station. Her face hurt, as she forced herself to smile.

"You can stop pretending now," Father Molloy said gently. "She can't see you anymore."

"I have no idea…" Mrs. Grey stopped at the look in his eye. "All right, yes I am worried. I think Denver is a good place for Wilma to go, but I am scared it will be too much for her."

He offered her his arm, which she took, as they walked back toward town.

"What's in Denver?"

Mrs. Grey hesitated. She didn't want to break Wilma's confidence but at the same time she needed some reassurance she was doing the right thing. "There is a lady called Eliza Jane Brown. Her mother was Clara Brown. Have you heard of her?"

"No, should I have?"

"Guess not. Clara was an ex-slave who spent the last years of her life trying to reunite slave families. You know how often slaves were sold at auction and whole families could be separated. Then the war came and even more were torn from their loved ones. This lady felt very strongly someone should try to help people locate their loved ones. She was looking for her family. She found her daughter Eliza Jane."

"You want to introduce Wilma to Clara to help her find her parents and siblings?"

Mrs. Grey bit her lip uncertain how to answer as she didn't want to lie.

"Clara is dead now but her daughter, Eliza Jane, has retained her mother's contacts. There might be someone who knew Wilma when she was a slave and can help piece together her family history."

"You are a wonderful lady, Mrs. Grey. When I think how scared I was of you when I first arrived in Clover Springs."

"You! Scared of me? I don't believe it."

"Whether or not you believe it, it's true. I was absolutely terrified of you, and make no mistake, you were and still are a force to be reckoned with in this town. You hide it well under that crusty exterior but you have a heart of gold."

"Father Molloy, you are embarrassing both of us," she retorted despite being very pleased at his compliment. "I best go and tell Wilma she is going to Denver."

"You mean ask her, don't you?"

"I most certainly do not. She is going to Denver whether she wants to or not. I am not letting her stay in bed a minute longer."

Father Molloy let out a roar of laughter causing people in the street to turn and look at them curiously. "That's the true Mrs. Grey in action."

She blushed scarlet as people continued to stare. "Good day, Father."

She marched up to the orphanage door, knocked and let herself in. She threw a quick hello in Samuel's direction before making her way to Wilma's bedroom.

"Wilma, get up. We are going to Denver."

"Why? I don't want to leave Clover Springs. I is happy here."

"It's not forever. We are going on vacation. Come along now. I have the tickets booked. We leave tomorrow."

"Vacation. I ain't going."

"Yes, you are. There is an ex-slave in Denver named Eliza Jane, her mother Clara Brown died three years ago. Have you ever heard of her?"

"No."

Mrs. Grey ignored Wilma's attempt to appear disinterested. "You should have. She spent her whole free life trying to reunite ex-slaves with their families. There are lots of people like you, who were separated from their parents, siblings, or children."

"But you said she done died."

"Yes, but her daughter is alive and well. She may have some contacts. It's worth a try. You have a choice my friend, stay here and sulk in bed all day or get up and do something about finding your daughter."

Mrs. Grey hoped her no-nonsense tone would make Wilma angry. She wanted her old friend back. The one who would have hopped out of bed and stood opposite her with her hands on her hips while giving her a piece of her mind. She was disappointed. Wilma simply turned in the bed presenting Mrs. Grey with her back.

"Don't you dare ignore me. I am not going anywhere until you get out of that bed."

"You'll be waiting."

"I haven't got anything else to do apart from meet with Ma Kelley. She had some ideas about what to do with the orphans."

Wilma shot up in the bed. "Don't you let that old crow near my babies…" Wilma stopped mid-sentence. "You did that on purpose, didn't you?"

Mrs. Grey nodded, eyes twinkling. "I knew something had to get your attention. Always count on your love for other people." Mrs. Grey took Wilma's hand in hers. "I know you are scared. I know it could be painful. But isn't it worth a try?"

Wilma nodded slowly.

"I will be with you every step of the way. You are not alone. I promise."

"Why are you doing this?"

Mrs. Grey didn't wipe the tear away as it rolled down her cheek. "I need to help you find your daughter. I can still see the faces of those families my father sold at auction."

"You wasn't responsible for that."

"No, but I could have done more. I should have tried to stop him. Instead, I was too busy thinking of myself." Mrs. Grey grasped Wilma's hand tighter. "Please let me help you find your family."

Wilma took her time to answer. "We will go to Denver and meet with this lady. What will I tell everyone?"

"What do you want to say? We can tell them we are taking a small vacation. Nobody needs to know anything else. But it's up to you."

* * *

Wilma packed in silence while thoughts raced around her head. Would this Eliza Jane woman be able to help? Could Solace be alive? Would she recognize her if she was? Would her daughter want to know her, especially given the life she had lived?

A knock on the door interrupted her thoughts.

"Can I come in, please, Miss Wilma?"

"Course you can, Rosa. I've missed your smile."

Rosa threw her arms around Wilma nearly knocking her to the ground.

"I thought you were going to die. I am so glad you didn't."

"Me too, Rosa. I am sorry you were so worried, but I ain't going nowhere."

Rosa looked confused. "Mrs. Grey said you was going on vacation. You are going to bring me back a present."

Wilma sat on the bed indicating Rosa should sit beside her.

"Yes, I'm going to Denver for a couple of days, but I will be back."

"I'll miss you but I like the idea of a present."

Wilma laughed. "I'll get you something special. Now tell me how is school?"

"We ain't got our new teacher yet. I met her outside the store. She seems nice but she talks funny. She doesn't talk like you or me. Not like Mrs. Grey either. She sounds like she has something in her mouth when she's speaking. And her clothes, you ain't never seen nothing like them."

Wilma smiled at the child. Rosa was obsessed with

clothes and planned to be a dressmaker when she grew up. She had talent too. Wilma wondered what her parents had worked as. She guessed, given the circumstances, they were unlikely to ever find out.

CHAPTER 18

Eleanor came downstairs to find Martha fixing something to eat.

"I just bumped into Ellen at the store, she asked can you wait to start school until Monday? I am not sure why."

"I can wait. I am sure she has her reasons." Eleanor tried to sound confident but she was worried her past may have caught up with her. Should she seek Ellen out and ask her? But that would look suspicious if the delay had nothing to do with her. She was so preoccupied she took a few minutes to realize Martha was upset.

"What's wrong? Please tell me."

"My grandchildren are ill, the ones who live outside town."

"Oh no, poor things. Are you going to see them?" Eleanor asked.

"I hate to leave you alone, especially when you are new in town but my daughter needs me. She is pregnant and cannot cope with her sick children. If I had any other—"

"Please, Mrs. Sullivan, I mean Martha. I will be fine. Go be with your daughter. Take as long as you need."

"Katie, the lady at the store, is my daughter-in-law. You can always ask her if you need anything."

"I will. But I am sure I will be fine." Eleanor tried her best to convince both of them.

"Thank you. You are such a kind person. Clover Springs has been lucky again." Martha went off to pack a bag leaving Eleanor behind. She looked around the room. She couldn't help wishing she'd had a mother who would drop everything to help her. How she could do with someone now. But there was nobody. Her mother had died long ago, her father was dead now and her relations, she still considered them her family despite what they did, weren't interested. She could be dead for all they cared. In fact, it would probably suit them better if she was. No chance of any further scandal encroaching on their social lives.

Eleanor choked back a sob. She couldn't give in to tears. Not today. Mrs. Sullivan would think it was over her leaving and then she might not go. Today, it was time for the stiff upper lip the British were so famous for. Except she wasn't British not really. Not anymore.

* * *

Eleanor screamed as the back door burst open admitting Gary Barrett. "Oh, it's you. Sorry, Mrs. Sullivan didn't tell me she was expecting callers."

"She wasn't. I happened to walk by and saw the smoke and thought you might need some help." He moved past her quickly to remove the remains of the dish from the stove.

"Thank you, but it's not necessary. I can manage."

"Looks like it," he commented as his gaze took in the mess in the usually pristine kitchen.

Her nostrils flared at his sarcasm. He took a deep breath before saying in a much nicer voice. "It's obvious something went wrong. What can I do?"

"You can leave. I will be fine once I get the hang of the stove. It's different to the one I used back ho…in England."

He noticed the slip and the pain in her eyes.

"Miss Templeton, I know we got off on the wrong foot. It was totally my fault. I also know you have never used a stove before."

"How can you tell that?"

"Well, you usually put the wood on top of the paper for a start with the coal added after when the fire has caught."

"Oh," she whispered and confirmed everything.

"I guess you have never prepared your own meals before, have you?"

"No. Before you jump to conclusions I wasn't spoilt but my fam…relatives had servants. They did everything and made it look so easy too. I am useless." She sat down at the table.

"What were you trying to do?"

"I thought I could cook some dinner. I can't find a café in town and there is no hotel."

"What have you eaten since Mrs. Sullivan left yesterday?"

Eleanor noted he knew about her landlady. It was a really small town if everyone's comings and goings were so well known. Had she picked the right place to hide? He was staring at her. She blurted, "Sandwiches. She left some bread and there was ham and some pickles. She also left some cake and cookies."

"You must be starving. Why didn't you cook some eggs?"

"I tried but the shell ended up in the pan and then it all stuck, and oh what's the use, I am not suited to living out here miles away from civilization. I should have moved to a city where they have restaurants and…and…hotels."

"Calm down. I can show you how to cook some eggs. It isn't hard. In no time, you will be cooking lots of things."

"Aren't you busy?"

"No, the saloon is always quiet in the mornings. Anyway, no one will die if they don't get a drop of whiskey, will they?"

She half-smiled.

"Coffee?" he suggested.

"It's in that jar over there but…well, the bits are bigger than they were in England. It tastes funny."

This time he had to turn away to hide his smile. Did you grind them?"

She shook her head miserably.

"Let's start slowly. You get the coffee beans and I will fill up the pan with water. We will both feel better after some coffee. Now does Mrs. Sullivan keep hens or does she get her eggs from the store?"

"I think from the store but I don't know. I haven't seen any hens."

He grinned as she looked around her as if expecting hens to walk across the kitchen floor. She was right, she didn't know anything about cooking. But it was okay. He knew enough to teach her the basics. It was the perfect chance to spend some time with her and get to know the person behind the beautiful mask.

* * *

He cooked her dinner and she insisted he join her. She knew she would never have done so if they were in England but for once the rules could go out the window. She was lonely, hated eating by herself and he had fixed dinner. They talked about all sorts of things. He was so easy to speak too. She guessed he was used to chatting about everything and nothing due to his saloon.

"Why does a man who doesn't drink own a saloon?" she asked after he said he hated the taste of alcohol.

"I'm not really qualified for anything else. I am not a farmer and don't know one end of a horse from the other so my employment prospects were rather narrow. I didn't enjoy school much either, and I hated working underground in the mines."

"I thought you would have loved school. You know so much about different things."

"I love to read and to learn but let's just say me and teachers didn't get along too well."

Eleanor laughed as he realized who he was talking

to. "I didn't have teachers like you. I mean they were old and boring and…"

"You didn't offend me, Mr. Barrett, so please stop."

He smiled his thanks. The smile lasted as she found she couldn't tear her eyes from his. She had an urge to move closer to him. Instead, she stood and started clearing the plates. She needed to occupy herself.

"Thank you very much for the company, but I best get going. Good night, Miss Templeton."

"Thank you and goodnight."

She closed the door behind him and leaned against it. He was the most interesting person she had ever spoken too. If she was honest, it wasn't only his mind that attracted her. He wasn't polished or groomed like the men she was used to, but he seemed more real. He had lovely eyes and a nice smile. He didn't have whiskers either. She hated facial hair. What was she doing? There was no point in thinking about him romantically, only heartache came from that. And she'd had her heart broken enough already.

CHAPTER 19

Bright and early Monday morning, Eleanor knocked on the door of the school house. As she waited for an answer, she smoothed down her dress and checked her hat was still straight. Her palms were all sweaty. She hoped her gloves wouldn't feel wet when she shook their hands. What would they be like?

The door opened as a young lady carrying a baby stood smiling at her.

"I'm sorry to keep you waiting. I shouted to come in but I don't think you heard me."

"No, I'm sorry. I didn't," Eleanor said quietly.

"Come inside. Laura will be back any minute. My name is Ellen, Ellen Higgins."

"Nice to meet you, Mrs. Higgins."

"Oh, call me Ellen, please. We are all equals here. I imagine its very different from what you are used to."

"Why do you say that?" Eleanor's tone caused Ellen's eyes to widen. "What I mean is what do you think I am used to?" Eleanor's heart was beating rapidly making breathing a little difficult. If she kept this up they would march her out of town.

"I only meant Clover Springs is very different from what I saw when I went to college. I imagine an English school is very caught up on structure and who is the most senior teacher. Isn't it like that?"

"Oh my yes, totally. You can only sit on a certain chair if you have been with the school for one hundred years."

Ellen smiled, her smile lighting up her whole face.

"I like that you have a sense of humor, with some of our children you will need one. Oh, there's Laura now."

Her sense of unease was back. What if Laura wasn't as nice as Ellen?

"Laura Kelley, this is Miss Templeton." Ellen turned to Eleanor. "I forgot to ask you your first name."

"Eleanor. Nice to meet you, Mrs. Kelley."

The red-haired girl smiled, her eyes kind. Eleanor's nerves floated away.

"Oh please, don't call me that. You obviously

haven't had the pleasure of meeting my mother-in-law yet. Although she will love you."

Eleanor wasn't sure whether to be pleased or not by the comment as it didn't sound like Mrs. Kelley was someone she wanted to meet. Her face must have reflected her thoughts as Ellen hastened to add.

"What Laura meant was Ma Kelley as we call her, has a certain idea of what a young lady should look like. You would match that to perfection. Your clothes are wonderful. I assume they are the latest fashion?" Ellen asked as she took Eleanor's hand and drew her into the classroom, the baby held firmly in the other one.

"Well, in England they would be quite new, but I don't know what the fashions are like here. I haven't been to any of your shops. Despite my clothes, I have to watch my pennies. Hence, why I am here."

"We are all very glad you are here. Both Ellen and I had babies recently, and we have found the job even more tiring than usual," Laura said indicating Eleanor should take a seat.

"We have also had a large number of new children to cater for." Ellen explained how the orphans had been rescued on the train. "We have so many children it would be nice to separate them into groups based on age and perhaps ability. But until the school is expanded, we have to make do."

"It's lovely and cozy in here," Eleanor complimented the two ladies.

"We try but it can sometimes get very cold, especially in winter. We make the children take turns at the stove. You won't have experienced anything like our winters. I believe the weather in England is fairly mild."

"We don't tend to have blizzards and other extreme conditions like you do here. The story of those poor school children dying in January scared me, I must admit."

"We read some of the stories in the newspaper. Some of the children brought some stories to school too. Some of them true and others that have been disproved as rumors. But a lot of people, mainly children, died," Laura said.

"Yes, it was so tragic. Their parents must have been frantic," Ellen added. "We are lucky here in Clover Springs. We escaped the worst of the weather at least so far. I believe you are staying with Martha Sullivan. She is my sister's mother-in-law. Such a lovely lady."

"She has been very kind to me," Eleanor said quietly.

"You will have to come out to the ranch and meet the rest of the ladies. We tend to meet at Mary's as she has the biggest place. Not to mention the secret weapon being Mrs. Higgins to cook for us."

Eleanor's head was buzzing with the names of all the people she had to meet.

"Don't worry about remembering who is who. You will know everyone soon enough. Clover Springs is so small, everyone knows everyone else," Ellen said reassuringly.

"Do you have any questions you wanted to ask me?" Eleanor hoped her voice didn't betray her nerves.

"Not really. Father Molloy is happy with your credentials. He says we are lucky to have someone so well qualified. I assume you have taught boys as well as girls," Laura said, looking down at some paperwork on the desk.

"Actually, I haven't." Both women looked at her. "I have only taught girls and that was only for a few months. I worked as a governess rather than a teacher. I hope that won't change your mind."

"Not at all, although you are in for a baptism of fire." Laura exchanged a glance with Ellen. "Our boys are mostly well-behaved but we have a couple of little horrors. You will have to put them in their place. Any signs of weakness and they will torment you making your life, and ours, miserable."

"Do you cane them?" Eleanor shuddered even saying the words. She had never used any form of corporal punishment on a child, although she'd been the victim of it more than once.

"No, never. Neither of us believe in corporal punishment. You must agree never to resort to it either," Laura said firmly.

"That's easy. I hate it too."

"Good, I think you will fit in here very well. Bertram Shaw is likely to give you some lip over your, well you know…" Ellen's voice trailed off.

Eleanor's stomach hit the floor. Had Father Molloy told them her history? Did it make them think less of her?"

"What Ellen means is your beautiful accent. It is so different from what we are used to. You sound like I imagine Queen Victoria does."

"Oh no, she has a much nicer voice than mine," Eleanor said without thinking.

"You met the Queen?" Ellen stammered.

Drat it anyway, why did she have to say anything. She looked at the two ladies who were now staring at her, their faces lit up with excitement.

"Yes, I was presented at court. It's quite usual in England. It doesn't mean anything." Flustered, Eleanor attempted to make light of it.

"Yes, it does. I read about it in the society pages when I lived in New York."

"Oh, you must come to tea and tell us all about it. The ladies will be interested. Although many of us are Irish, we are still fascinated by the workings of the royal court. We may not want a British government in Ireland, but we are feminine enough to like the beautiful gowns and jewelry worn by ladies of the court."

"It was nothing. The Prince of Wales insisted it happen, but in reality they only allowed it as my father saved his life when he toured India. I didn't have the correct background to be presented. I am not a fan of the season. It is a marriage market, pure and simple."

Eleanor kicked herself, she had only made the whole thing worse by making the season even more interesting. Why did she have to mention the queen?

She stood up. "I better be getting back to the boarding house, and you two will want to return to your families. Do I start tomorrow?"

"Yes, please. Ellen will be here in the morning, and I will take over after lunch. It will be lovely working with you, Eleanor. I hope you will like it here," Laura said kindly.

"Thank you. I am sure I will."

Eleanor shook their hands and walked as quickly as she could, without appearing rude, out of the school and toward the boarding house. Now she had really done it. She could see the questions in their faces. Why would anyone who had met the queen want to settle as a teacher in the back end of nowhere? Why indeed?

* * *

As she walked, her thoughts turned back to that special night. Father had insisted on buying the most beautiful Worth dress. He'd lent her the family diamond earrings to wear telling her Grandmamma had approved. The old lady hadn't but she wasn't to know that until much later after her beloved father had died.

Her father had introduced her to so many wonderful people. His friends from the army and from his work in America. She'd been so excited, she hadn't noticed the frowns and little comments from people. Prince Bertie as he was known had taken a liking to her and insisted she be presented. Her father had accompanied him on his tour of India. They were good friends.

Eleanor didn't want to think of her father anymore. It was too painful trying to reconcile the wonderful man she had known with the real one who had lied to her. She was frowning as she walked into the boarding house hating the thoughts of being alone again. But she got a pleasant surprise.

"Are you all right, Miss Templeton?"

"Yes, perfectly fine. Thank you, Mrs. Sullivan, you are back. I am so pleased to see you. How are the children?"

"You don't look it. You look rather cross," Mrs.

Sullivan replied, her eyes full of concern. "I hope people are being kind to you."

"Yes, everyone is very nice. Sorry, I was thinking about something. Nothing to do with Clover Springs. I met both Laura and Ellen. They were lovely. But how are your grandchildren? I hope you didn't rush back on my account."

"Not at all," Mrs. Sullivan said, although she spoke so quickly Eleanor thought she might be lying. "The children are much better now and my daughter said it was time for me to go home. We love each other dearly but sometimes two women in one kitchen can be one woman too much."

Eleanor laughed politely. She'd never experienced anything domestic. She thought it might be fun but bowed to Mrs. Sullivan's greater experience.

"I am so glad you met both Ellen and Laura. Two wonderful girls. I am guessing you have been through some hard times."

At the look of terror on Eleanor's face, Mrs. Sullivan quickly continued.

"I am not asking what happened nor do I know anything but I have a daughter. I learned over the years to read her like a book. You will be fine in Clover Springs. Better than that. You will be happy. Take your time to settle in and give the town a chance. It is special. Many a broken heart has been cured here."

Eleanor was about to protest it wasn't a man who'd made her heart break but she stopped herself in time. Wasn't it better people thought she had run from a broken romance than know the real reason?

"Thank you, Mrs. Sullivan. I am very tired so I am going to bed. Goodnight."

"Don't you want some tea?"

"No thank you." Craving her bed and some privacy, Eleanor walked slowly up the stairs.

CHAPTER 20

"She looks incredibly sad and lost, doesn't she?" Ellen said as she cleaned the slates in preparation for the next day.

"Yes, Ellen, she does but I am not sure she wants us to do anything about it. She got quite prickly, didn't she?" Laura asked as she walked down the boardwalk to the orphanage. Paul was waiting to bring her home.

"I think that's the whole British stiff upper lip thing. I didn't come across it much in Ireland being so young. But I remember my mam telling us stories about the ladies at the big house and how they had to pretend everything was all right even if it wasn't. Like when their brother was killed fighting some war, there was no wailing or gnashing of teeth."

"I am sure they cried, or do you think they are heartless because they are British?"

Ellen poked Laura in the ribs. "That's not fair. Not every Irish person hates the British."

"Well, you aren't too fond of them. Not since they sent Liam to prison."

"True, but that's not Miss Templeton's fault," Ellen said sighing as she thought of Liam. "But going back to the ladies of the big house, if someone died in Ireland we would all be crying for days. They even pay old ladies to do the crying on behalf of the family. You haven't seen anything like it."

"I went to a couple of wakes back in Boston, but I guess nothing like what you are describing. I wonder what caused Miss Templeton's distress. She can't be afraid of us, can she?"

"Well, you can be quite frightening when you want to be, Mrs. Kelley."

This time it was Laura who gave Ellen a dig in the ribs. They were laughing as they pushed the door open to the orphanage.

"You two are in great form this evening," Samuel Higgins commented.

"Aren't we always?" Ellen asked her husband.

"I am not going to answer that. I like living," Samuel replied.

"I love you, too, dear!" Ellen retorted but she had a smile on her face.

"How is Wilma?"

"Better actually. Mrs. Grey was here for ages today. Rosa said they are going on a trip to Denver."

"What's in Denver?" Ellen and Laura asked at the same time.

"Can I go up and see her?"

"Laura, you don't need to ask. Go on. I will make us a cup of coffee and bring it up," Ellen said. "Just as soon as I give Jake a cuddle and a kiss."

"What was the new teacher like? Will she fit in?" Samuel asked.

Ellen took a second or two to answer. "Yes, I think she will but it may take some time. She is very different to us. She's British and..."

"You haven't held that against her, have you?"

"Not you as well. Why does anyone think I would do that? I don't blame the entire British population for what happened to my mam and my brother. Miss Templeton wasn't in Galway, and I doubt she even knows where it is." Ellen also spoke fast when she was annoyed.

"All right, keep your hair on. What's wrong with her then?"

"There's nothing wrong with her as you so nicely put it. She's just very different. For one thing, how many people do you know who met Queen Victoria?"

The two men exchanged glances.

"See. Exactly what I was thinking."

"So she's met the Queen of England. I'm sure that's relatively easy given she lived in England," Paul Kelley said shrugging his shoulders.

"No, it's not actually, unless you are a member of the aristocracy," Ellen said trying not to sound smug.

"You mean the rumors are true, she is a real lady?" he asked.

"Who's been spreading rumors?" Ellen couldn't believe someone was already spreading gossip about their new teacher. She'd only been in Clover Springs a couple of days.

"Charlie Staunton. He reckons he is going to ask her out."

"Charlie Stanton and Miss Templeton. That is never going to happen."

Ellen followed Laura up the stairs carrying a tray of coffees. The thought of Charlie Staunton and Eleanor Templeton together making her laugh.

To her surprise, Wilma was sitting up in bed, her hand clasped in Laura's.

"You got a wide smile on your face, Miss Ellen. So nice to see."

"I was just laughing at something Paul said," Ellen explained turning to look at Laura. "Seems Charlie Staunton thinks he has a chance with Miss Templeton."

Laura burst out laughing. "Oh, I would love to see

him try. He'll get frostbite if she turns her cold voice on him."

"Who is this?"

"Miss Eleanor Templeton, our new teacher. She's ever so nice. A real lady."

"Laura's not joking. She's been presented to Queen Vitoria."

"What is she doing in Clover Springs?"

"No idea, Wilma. She seems quite sad. In fact, if you were feeling better, we would be sending her to see you for one of your chats."

Ellen's heart beat faster at the look of panic on Wilma's face. What was wrong with her old friend? In the past, she would have been the first one to help a newcomer to their town. Now she looked terrified.

"Don't worry, Wilma, we won't be bringing her or any other stranger here. Not until you are fully better. What's this trip you are going on?" Ellen asked trying to get rid of the panic in Wilma's eyes.

Wilma's expression turned guarded making Ellen and Laura exchange glances.

"Mrs. Grey thinks it would do me good to take a trip, so we decided to go and see Denver. She says there is plenty to do there. We can stay in hotel and see some plays maybe even a circus."

"I thought you were supposed to be resting," Laura chided gently.

"I'll rest long enough when I is dead," Wilma replied sharply.

Ellen caught the glisten of tears in Laura's eyes before her friend turned her face. She looked back at Wilma seeing the sadness in hers. She'd never heard Wilma speak so harshly to anyone, least of all Laura. When would her friend be back to normal?

CHAPTER 22

The morning sun rose bright in the sky despite it only being March. Eleanor shivered as she got out of bed, her stomach swirling with excitement. She couldn't wait to start teaching. Although she hadn't been a governess long, she had loved the experience. Children were so open minded and in most cases very willing to learn once you found a way to interest them.

She dressed quickly planning to have a cup of coffee and leave for the school. She wanted to make a good impression. But her landlady had other ideas. When she opened her bedroom door, the smell of frying bacon wafted its way up the stairs. Her stomach rumbled in response making her thankful nobody was standing nearby. She walked down the stairs carefully as they were a little steep. Mrs. Sullivan was standing by the stove, a skillet of bacon and eggs ready for serving.

"Good morning, Miss Templeton. I thought you'd need a good breakfast before you take on that lot at school."

"Please call me Eleanor, and you make it sound as if I am off to war."

"No, not at all." Martha Sullivan smiled. "War would be easier."

Eleanor giggled. It had been a long time since anyone cared for her welfare. As in really cared, not just done things because they were paid to do it as the servants in her father's house had done.

"What can I do to help?"

"Nothing, dear. Do you mind eating in the kitchen? The other rooms are rather chilly."

"Not at all, it's cozy in here."

"Take a seat then, dear, and pour us both a cup of coffee. Or do you prefer tea?"

"Coffee is lovely, thank you. You are very kind to get up and do this."

"I am not being kind. I love being useful. At my age in life, when your children are grown, it gets, well, I guess you would call it lonesome. I love having some company. Female company that is." Mrs. Sullivan's cheeks turned pink making Eleanor see she must have been very pretty in her youth.

"Thank you anyway. I was just going to have some coffee and run."

"Believe me, dear, you will be glad of a good breakfast. It will sustain you for the day ahead."

"Are they really that bad? Ellen and Laura seemed to think they were good children."

"I am only teasing you, dear. The majority of them are lovely. The one you need to watch is Bertram Shaw. His mother has him ruined." Mrs. Sullivan crossed herself. "Best add that to my list of sins to confess, although I think Father Molloy will understand."

"He's very different, isn't he?" Eleanor saw the look of confusion on Mrs. Sullivan's face. "The priest I mean."

"To what?"

"Well, I'm not Catholic but we used to go to church sometimes and our vicar, well, he was rather sour. He never smiled or seemed happy about anything."

"Our Reverend Timmons is lovely and his wife is a real dear. But there is a priest who used to come to the town and let's just say he could be your vicar's brother. Father Molloy is special and we are lucky to have him."

"He was very kind to me," Eleanor murmured.

"Course he was. Aren't you a lovely young lass. Why would anyone be anything but kind."

Eleanor looked at Mrs. Sullivan's back as she

dished the breakfast onto plates. If only her family had people in it like this woman, she wouldn't be a million miles from home.

* * *

She didn't see anyone she recognized as she walked down the road. The people she did meet, smiled in greeting but kept walking. Pushing open the school house door, she saw Ellen had already arrived.

"Morning, Miss Templeton."

"Please call me Eleanor, Ellen."

"I will but not in front of the children," Ellen said with a smile on her face. "How are you feeling?"

"Excited and a little nervous. Your friend Mrs. Sullivan cooked me a large breakfast.

"Yes, you need to watch things with Martha. She will feed you up so much, your own mother won't recognize you."

At the mention of her mother, Eleanor looked away. Where was her mother? Was she really dead or had that been a lie as well. Thankfully, Ellen was distracted by the arrival of some of the children.

"Take your seats children, I want our new teacher to see how well behaved you all are."

"Yes, Miss Ellen," they chorused.

"Many of the children live at the orphanage and it

was too cumbersome for them to remember to call me Mrs. Higgins at school and Miss Ellen at home. So we decided on Miss Ellen," Ellen explained.

"What do they call Laura?"

"Miss Laura but that is because Laura refuses to answer to Mrs. Kelley. She has her reasons which will become apparent when you meet her in-laws. What would you like to be called?"

"I think Miss Eleanor, if that is all right with you? I don't like to be different."

Ironic really, given who she really was, but she wasn't about to explain that to Ellen.

"I will introduce you just as soon as they are all sitting down. They may ask you a few questions. Just answer the ones you want to and ignore the rest. Although I love living here, it is a small town and we rarely get to meet people from other places."

Eleanor nodded, her attention taken by the sheer numbers of children coming to school. How on earth would she mange all of them?

"The older ones help so don't look so worried you will be fine. We are here to help you settle in."

"Thank you for being so kind to me."

"My pleasure. I hope we will become good friends." Ellen gave her arm a squeeze before going to help a small child take off her coat.

Eleanor looked around at the classroom again. One

boy was staring at her, almost rudely. She turned away from him hoping he would stop but when she glanced back, his gaze was still fixed on her.

"Is something wrong?" she asked him, expecting him to redden or at least show some sign of embarrassment but he kept staring.

"Bertram Shaw, Miss Eleanor asked you a question."

"I was just wondering was it true? What they said about her?"

Eleanor gripped her hands together. They didn't know anything. Despite the way he was staring at her.

"Is what true may I ask?" She used her frostiest tone but it slid off him.

"Are you really a lady? Did you live in a big castle and are you friends with the Prince of Wales?"

"Yes, no, and my father was," she said thinking as she was female, she was a lady despite not being a member of the aristocracy.

His facial expression made it very difficult not to laugh. Ellen had to turn away, her shoulders shaking with laughter which didn't help. But Eleanor was determined this boy was not going to ruin her first day at her new job.

"Anything else?" she demanded as if addressing a servant in her father's home.

"No."

"No, what?" She glared at him until he looked down at his feet.

"No, Miss Eleanor."

"Take a seat please and open your book." Her tone brooked no argument and he sat down quietly. She looked over his head to see Ellen giving her the thumbs-up.

Round one to her but she was convinced she hadn't heard the last of Master Shaw.

CHAPTER 21

Wilma and Mrs. Grey stood at the station waiting for the train. They had refused all offers from people eager to see them off. They were nervous enough and didn't want anyone commenting on how scared they seemed to be going on a vacation. The train arrived on time and they duly took their seats. There weren't many people traveling and they had the entire car to themselves.

"You should have seen the look on Doc's face when I told him I was going on a trip."

"I knew he'd be upset. What did he say?" Wilma asked.

"He reminded me Doc Erin was away."

"As if you could have forgotten that. But maybe he was right. We should have delayed our trip," Wilma said, biting her lip.

"Absolutely not. I told him in the sweetest voice I could find that he hadn't always valued my services so highly."

Wilma burst out laughing. She knew Doc had once found Mrs. Grey to be bossy and irritating. She was still bossy but he knew she was usually right. She was a great organizer.

"I suggested a vacation would give him time to value me properly."

Mrs. Grey looked so serious Wilma wasn't sure she was joking.

"But then I gave him the cake I'd asked Mrs. Higgins to make. You know what his stomach is like," Mrs. Grey grinned at Wilma. "Emer reminded me how much he'd enjoyed all the cakes delivered when she was in his care that time she was supposed to be in prison."

"I nearly feel sorry for the poor doctor with you women scheming around him."

"Don't waste your pity. He loves it. Anyway, Emer has promised to spoil him rotten until we get back. Mrs. Higgins said she wants to come the next time we go on vacation. I promised she could."

"Emer is an excellent nurse so Doc will be fine. So where are we going next time?"

"I have no idea. We will throw a pin on a map and just go. Wouldn't it be fun?" Mrs. Grey asked.

Wilma didn't answer. She wasn't at all sure she was young and fit enough to enjoy what Mrs. Grey would view as fun.

They settled back into their seats, trying to get comfortable each content with the silence between them. Sometime later, Wilma woke up. She stretched her neck, having a crick in it from lying in the wrong position.

"Do you think we should have let Father Molloy accompany us? Denver is a big city." Mrs. Grey asked as they watched the passing scenery through the window.

"What you scared of? Father Molloy couldn't help us if we got in trouble. He's older than me."

"Yes, but he's a man, Wilma."

"Hate to break it to you, Mrs. Grey, but I don't think anyone will want to carry us off. Our virtue be safe."

Mrs. Grey stared at Wilma for a few seconds before she laughed.

"That's the first time in a long time you sounded like my friend Wilma. Welcome back."

Wilma smiled but inside her heart was beating really quickly. What would they find in Denver? What if her daughter was still alive but didn't want to see her. Could she deal with that pain? But at least she would know.

"Stop it right now."

"I ain't doing nothing," Wilma protested but Mrs. Grey was looking at her in her knowing way.

"You are worrying about what might happen. You can't do that. You've told us often enough, we can only deal with what we know right now."

"Stop lecturing me. You start doing that again, I is going home. You can go on this wild goose chase on your own."

Mrs. Grey clapped her hands, a giant smile on her face. "I knew you were in there somewhere. This is going to be fun, my friend. A few days away, just the two of us, is just the ticket we needed."

"Hmmm." Wilma wasn't convinced. What if this Eliza woman wouldn't talk to Mrs. Grey because of her past? Weren't many ex-slaves who associated with the daughters of plantation owners.

"I know they may treat me with suspicion," Mrs. Grey said smiling as if she read Wilma's mind every day. "But we will deal with that if it happens. Now our train is here. Let's enjoy ourselves too. It's been a long time since I had a vacation."

The train journey passed relatively smoothly until another traveler entered the car, taking a seat near them. He kept staring over at the two of them but they did their best to ignore him. It didn't work.

He couldn't keep his outrage hidden for long.

"I do not believe the train company allows maids to travel in the first-class car."

"Can't see why not. They let you travel in this car, don't they? I assumed it was for ladies and gentlemen only but obviously not."

The man blustered but didn't get a word in as Mrs. Grey continued speaking in a voice full of concern. "Where is this unfortunate maid you are so worried about?" Mrs. Grey looked around the car as if genuinely trying to locate a maid.

Wilma wanted to laugh at the expression on the man's face but she daren't. She simply stared at him until he moved to another seat. Only then, did she and Mrs. Grey dissolve into a fit of giggles like two young school girls. Tears were running freely down their faces before they recovered their composure.

"Oh, Lorena, I think you are right. We needed to get away from Clover Springs for a while." Wilma didn't notice she'd called Mrs. Grey by her first name.

"You certainly did, my friend. You always take everyone else's cares and woes on your shoulders. It's time for you to look after yourself for a while."

"Thank you, Mrs. Grey."

"For heaven's sake, Wilma, will you call me Lorena. We are the best of friends. Aren't we?"

Wilma squeezed her friend's hand, her voice having left her.

CHAPTER 22

Mrs. Grey had booked them a nice hotel not too far from where Eliza Jane lived. Wilma ignored the looks the receptionist gave her. She had the same right to stay in the hotel as anyone else. She adopted Alicia's method of dismissing anyone who was rude by looking down her nose at them. It made her smile inside to see their surprise at her reaction. If they thought they were going to ruin her day with their petty remarks or dirty looks, they were sadly mistaken.

"I think we both should take a nap to get our energy back after that trip. I had forgotten how hard the seats in train cars are," Lorena Grey suggested.

Wilma guessed Mrs. Grey was trying to make sure she didn't overdo it. Doc Erin had left strict instructions that Wilma was not to get involved in anything strenuous.

"That sounds like a good idea. Will we meet down here at eight for dinner?"

"Good plan. I hope you rest, my dear friend."

Wilma was sure she wouldn't. Her mind was going over and over the last time she had seen her daughter. What would Eliza Jane know? Maybe she wouldn't be able to help them at all. But if she was, what would she uncover. Poking at the past didn't always result in good news. She knew that better than anyone. What if they found her daughter and she didn't want to know? Would she be able to cope with the pain of rejection?

Shoulders slumped, she walked into her room not noticing the beauty of her surroundings.

"Can I get you anything, ma'am?" a pretty young maid asked.

"No thank you. I am going to rest for a while."

"Good idea, traveling is hard on everyone." The girl smiled as she left the room. Wilma stared at her, wondering if she was as happy as she seemed. Did she have a family close by? What was it like to work somewhere where the staff believed people like them were inferior? Funny how everyone had thought the Civil War would end prejudice. It hadn't. In some ways, it had made it worse. She had met her fair share of Yankees who blamed her kind for the fact the war had been fought in the first place. If they hadn't been slaves they wouldn't have needed to fight. It wasn't as if any of her people had woken up and decided they wanted to be enslaved. It wasn't their fault but some white people just didn't get that.

She lay on the bed, her mind twirling so fast, she got dizzy. Maybe taking a walk would make her feel better. She got up again and put her shoes on. It was time to see a little bit of Denver. Mrs. Grey was sleeping so what she didn't know wouldn't hurt her.

* * *

IT HAD BEEN a long time since Wilma had walked the streets of a big city. She'd forgotten the sheer number of people moving around. Everything was so much bigger, noisier, and if she was honest, more frightening than she remembered. She saw a small store and decided to look inside to see if she could find a small gift for Eliza Jane. She didn't know the woman but she still didn't want to arrive on her doorstep with nothing in her hand. As soon as she walked in, she knew she had made a mistake. Everyone turned to stare at her. The person she assumed to be the store owner, crossed his arms over his chest.

"We don't sell what you're looking for."

"I think you are mistaken, sir, I see many items of

interest to me," Wilma responded sharply, although her knees were knocking.

"I am not the one who is mistaken, girl."

The use of the slur made Wilma's temper rise. She smiled sweetly at the man.

"Thank you for the compliment. Tis many a year since I be called a young one. I will just take my time to pick out my gift for my friend."

She looked at some items on a stand close to the window, but her gaze caught the shocked look of the young maid, who had shown her to her room earlier, standing outside the store. She was holding a basket over her arm. She gestured at Wilma to come outside.

Wilma didn't want the owner to think he had got the better of her.

"Thank you for your time but I see you are correct. You don't stock the quality my friend would expect," she said smiling sweetly as his face turned purple at her insult. "Good day." She lifted her skirts and swept grandly out of the store leaving silence in her wake.

"Ma'am, you going to get in trouble if you try shopping around here. They don't like our sort." Agitated, the young maid almost hauled Wilma down the street. She was walking so fast Wilma struggled to keep up with her.

"But you are here," Wilma stammered before stopping.

"Yes, but they knows I work for the hotel. They don't mind us being maids or other workers, but if they think we believe we are the same as them, they get angry."

"I ain't scared," Wilma protested.

"Well, you should be."

"But slavery is over. We got our freedom and our equality," Wilma argued stubbornly.

"We got our freedom all right, but we ain't got equality. Not yet. Maybe it will come in time but for the moment, I need to take you back to the hotel. I don't want anyone to hurt you." Although the maid was speaking to her, her eyes were darting everywhere as if she expected an attack any second.

"What's your name?"

"Annie, ma'am."

"You is very kind to think of my welfare, Annie."

"Ma'am, how did you get to dress so nice and stay in such places?" Annie asked in a whisper. "I don't mean to be impertinent but that lady you're with. She say she is your friend but she be white."

"She is my friend and I am proud to be hers. She worked on the Underground Railroad many years ago. Before you were even born. She is a special lady. As to your other question, my friends gave me this trip as a present."

"They is nice. I wish I had me friends like that."

"Annie, if you have people around you who love you, that's all that matters. No amount of money can ever compensate for people who care. You remember that."

"Yes, ma'am."

Wilma smiled at her gently. The young girl didn't believe her, that much was obvious. But in time, she would learn the lesson the hard way. Suddenly feeling very tired, she walked quietly back with Annie to the hotel.

"Thank you, dear. I am very sorry if I interfered with your work."

"It was a pleasure, ma'am. I can't wait to tell my ma all about what you did at the store. That will make her laugh until her belly is sore."

Wilma returned to her room eager to avoid Lorena Grey spotting her. She'd had enough today without a lecture on top for not resting as she should. She lay on the bed but she couldn't sleep. The Civil War had been over for years, yet things weren't much better for her people. She'd read about the Ku Klux Klan in the South but hadn't realized there were people up North who felt the same way. She'd forgotten so much of her life in the city. Clover Springs had nurtured and protected her, but it had almost made her forget about the reality of life for many of her people. What could she do to help people like Annie?

CHAPTER 23

CLOVER SPRINGS

Eleanor walked home in quiet contemplation. The first day had gone well. A couple of the children had tested her, none so openly as Master Shaw but she'd handled them well. If only Grace could see her now. Her best friend wouldn't believe it. Eleanor wondered where Grace was. Her letters had been returned unopened but she didn't, she couldn't, believe her friend had forsaken her as well. Grace wasn't like that but her mother was. Lady Devon behaved as if everyone was a thoroughbred horse. She knew the family history of most in their set. If she didn't approve of someone she cut them dead. Everyone knew a snub from Lady Devon was the death knell of any chance of success in society. Lady Devon had always been really nice to her until her Grandmamma decided to tell everyone her background. After that, Lady Devon had insisted Grace stay away from her. Grace had sneaked out a couple of times before Eleanor left London but someone had spied on them and reported back. The result was a sudden tour of Europe for Grace—the season was over after all—and banishment from England for Eleanor. She'd been given a one-way ticket to America with a letter of introduction to Mrs. Gantley.

* * *

She was so engrossed in her thoughts she walked into a man coming her way. She dropped her reticule in the process. Bending down to pick it up, his scent made her eyes water.

"Good afternoon, Miss Templeton. My name is Charlie Staunton. You have two of my children in your class."

"Good afternoon. I have not yet learned the names of all my students, but I am sure they will be a pleasure to teach. I must..." her efforts to move away from him failed.

"I am so glad we bumped into each other. I must say it is a pleasure to have someone such as yourself in Clover Springs. I would love to—"

"Staunton, what are you doing gasbagging in the

streets? You were supposed to meet me fifteen minutes ago. I don't like to be kept waiting."

Eleanor knew the voice, it made the little hairs on the back of her neck stand up but not with fright. She sensed him coming closer. She couldn't remember the last time she'd been so aware of a man.

"Have you been drinking, Barrett? I didn't have any such appointment," Staunton protested.

"Yes you did, you made it last night, but you were in your cups so perhaps you have forgotten."

Eleanor caught Gary's wink and had to turn away. Mr. Staunton's cheeks were reddening and his chest was pushed even further out. She thought he might burst his waistcoat.

"Excuse me gentlemen you obviously have things to discuss. I must be on my way." She walked as quickly as her clothes allowed ignoring the protests of Mr. Staunton. She'd recognized him as one of those who had been talking about her the other day. She didn't want to get to know him any better. He reminded her of a few of her father's friends who had a reputation for harassing single females.

* * *

Gary watched her walk away. Had she had trouble at school? She looked so unhappy as she walked up the street. He wondered what was the truth behind her arriving in Clover Springs? He didn't care about the facts for the sake of gossip but he hated people being unhappy. He'd seen enough hard times and unhappiness in the slums he'd grown up in back in London. His ma was always cheerful though, no matter what happened. Even when his father had been killed, she insisted on being thankful he had died outright and not of his injuries some days later. He hadn't suffered any pain was her reasoning. It didn't seem right to him as a boy. He had idolized his father and losing him had been the most painful thing to happen. But now he understood better why his mum had taken that approach. She had to find a way to cope without the love of her life. She had a child to bring up. She couldn't afford to stop living despite it being what she wanted.

He wanted a love affair like his parents had. They were genuinely happy together despite not having much in the way of material goods. They'd known from the first time they met they were going to marry. So he believed in love at first sight. But while he might have feelings for Miss Eleanor, it was obvious she wasn't ready for love. Not yet. Maybe never but certainly not until she let go of all the pain she was carrying inside her. Maybe she'd let him be her friend. Yeah and maybe the heavens would pour down gold coins instead of rain. What was he thinking? Women, particularly attractive, single young ladies, didn't make friends with a man.

He turned his attention back to Staunton who was still spluttering about not having a meeting.

"My apologies, Mr. Staunton. Seems I was mistaken. Sorry for interfering with your day."

Gary tipped his hat at the outraged man before turning around and heading back to the saloon.

CHAPTER 24

DENVER

The next morning, Lorena Grey knocked at Wilma's room. "I asked for breakfast to be served in here. I thought it might be easier than sitting in the dining room. It gives us a chance to chat in private."

Wilma wasn't fooled. She knew her friend was trying to protect her and loved her for it. The slight unpleasantness at the hotel yesterday was nothing compared to what she had experienced in the shop, but Annie's views had made her look at it in a new light. Racism was alive and well in Denver. She wasn't hungry, and although she felt bad about wasting food, she couldn't touch the breakfast.

"I have rented us a small carriage. I thought it would be easier to drive over to Eliza Jane's address rather than having to walk through the crowds."

Wilma sent Mrs. Grey a look. "You is acting on Doc Erin's orders, ain't ye?" she asked before adding "Isn't that expensive?"

"Not really. We are on vacation remember. It's time to treat ourselves."

The young man Mrs. Grey had engaged to drive the carriage was smartly dressed and very polite. If he was taken aback at the address Mrs. Grey asked him to drive to, he didn't show it. They sat in silence for which Wilma was thankful. She was thankful she'd been unable to eat breakfast earlier as her stomach roiled with nerves. Judging by the look in her friend's face, she was just as nervous.

They pulled up outside a small house, in a rather poor neighborhood. Wilma watched as the children came over to the carriage. They were all barefoot despite the relatively cold weather. She wished she had worn some of her old clothes rather than the gowns purchased for this trip. She exchanged a look with Mrs. Grey. This was it. This was where their questions would be answered.

The driver assisted both of them out of the carriage.

"Do you want me to wait here, ma'am?"

"No thank you, go and have a break but please come back in two hours."

He tipped his hat to her.

Mrs. Grey took Wilma's arm. "I guess you are even more nervous than I am. We can prop each other up," she whispered.

Wilma saw someone had come out of the house. She guessed it to be Eliza Jane, although the girl didn't greet them. They walked slowly up to the door.

"You didn't tell us you was white."

Before Wilma or Mrs. Grey could respond an older woman came out. "Jane Clara Brown, don't you let me hear you being rude to our guests again. You was brought up better than that. Now get out of here."

The girl slinked away leaving the women feeling uncomfortable.

"I is sorry for my girl. She has a heart full of anger. Please come inside."

"Thank you, Miss Brown," Wilma replied. "My name is Wilma and this is my friend Mrs. Grey."

The lady nodded as she stood back to let them enter. Although small, it was kept scrupulously clean. Every surface looked as if it had been scrubbed down in anticipation of their visit, but Wilma had a feeling it always looked as smart.

"You have a lovely home. Thank you for agreeing to meet with us," Wilma said quietly.

"You are welcome. It's a pity ma died as she is the one who knew the most. I helped her where I could but Clara knew everyone."

"We are sorry for your loss," Wilma offered as Mrs. Grey seemed to have lost the ability to speak.

"Please sit down. Sarah will bring us some coffee and cookies later. I thought you might want to speak in private first."

"You are very kind," Wilma said giving Mrs. Grey a discrete kick.

"Thank you so much for seeing us. I apologize. I am a bit overwhelmed," Mrs. Grey murmured not sounding at all like her confident self. Wilma gave her a worried look but she was staring at her hands.

"What can I do to help? Your letter was a bit vague on the details."

"My letter?" Wilma asked curiously.

"I sent a letter to Miss Brown explaining what I knew of the circumstances, which wasn't a lot." Mrs. Grey looked at Miss Brown. "Although we have been friends for a long time, we haven't always been completely honest with each other."

"Or ourselves," Wilma piped up gripping Lorena's hand. "I had a daughter. Solace was her name. Near the end of the war, in early eighteen sixty-four a group of Yankee soldiers came onto the plantation where we was slaves."

"They rescued you?"

"Not really. They treated us much the same as the Southern boys had done. Solace's best friend was one of the young men they started beating up. She went to his aid. They didn't like that. So I…well, I was afraid for her so I struck one of them. It got their attention and I told Solace to run. I ain't seen her since."

Wilma was speaking to her knees at this point in the story, tears falling down her cheeks. She didn't notice Eliza getting up from her chair until she had taken her in her arms.

"You mustn't be upset. You gave your child a chance of freedom. Did they catch her? Was she killed?"

"I don't know. I was taken away that night and I never went back. I tried but, well, people warned me not to. They said things were worse in a lot of ways after the war ended. There were many angry people on both sides who blamed us."

"People still feel that way all these years later. As if we were to blame for wanting to live a free people. So you think Solace may have escaped with her man?"

"I hope so but I can't see how they could have. At that time, the South was crawling with soldiers. From what I could see, neither side cared much for us.

"Some people did. I am sure, Mrs. Grey, you knew some people like you who obviously see us as equals."

"I'm afraid I didn't always see you that way. I was born on a Southern plantation." Mrs. Grey faltered as fear and anger crossed with curiosity in Eliza's eyes.

"My daddy owned lots of slaves. I used to think he was a good owner as he didn't beat them or starve them. It wasn't until I was a little older, I realized there wasn't any such thing. He had families torn apart, keeping the male slaves for the fields and selling on the female slaves. I don't know how many men were kept from their wives or mothers from their children. I let it happen too." Mrs. Grey reached into her bag for a hanky. She tried to halt the flow of tears but couldn't. Wilma was about to take her into her arms when Eliza beat her to it.

"Mrs. Grey, I don't know you but I knows you is a good person. You have feelings. You couldn't do nothing with your daddy in charge. It wasn't like you were a man. Nobody listens to women, doesn't matter if they be black or white."

"Mrs. Grey worked with the Underground Railway," Wilma added as Mrs. Grey tried to regain her composure. "She taught her daddy's slaves to read and write. Then she helped them get free."

A sudden knocking at the door interrupted them. They all stared at the old man who pushed it open. Coming inside, his face lit up with the biggest smile Wilma had seen in a long time.

"It is you. I knows you anywhere. Missy Lorena. You was my master's little girl."

Mrs. Grey went white with shock as the old grey-haired man moved from the door toward her.

"I thought my ole eyes were deceiving me but you are her, ain't ye?" the man asked.

Mrs. Grey nodded.

"Do you remember me, Missy Lorena? I used to let you ride the horses. When the master wasn't around. You used to call me—" The old man didn't get to finish as Mrs. Grey interrupted him.

"Sammy? Is it really you?"

Wilma watched in surprise as Lorena practically threw herself into his arms. "I can't believe it's really you. You didn't get caught. I was told you had been."

"No, Mr. David he was a real good man. He took me to the North. I didn't go to Canada, I didn't want to be in a different country. I lived in hiding until the war was over and I knew I could come home. Only I never got to go home as there wasn't nothing there for me no more. My family was gone and nobody knew where you went. Did you run away with Mr. David?"

"No, Sammy, I was stupid. I let him go without me."

"But why? You was in love with him and he with you."

"I was young and foolish," Mrs. Grey sniffed. "I should have gone. My life would have been so different. David might be alive. I was so selfish."

"Aw, Missy Lorena, I don't think you were ever

that. You were always so kind. I owe you my life. You got to come meet my family. They wouldn't be here if it weren't for you. Can you come?"

Wilma smiled as Lorena looked at her for permission. "Off you go. I will be fine here with Eliza."

"Are you sure? I am supposed to be looking after you."

"Go on with you. I is fine. What could happen to me sitting here?" Wilma asked shooing Mrs. Grey out the door.

"Sammy is going to be talking about that for days. He done tole us about a young white lady who helped him escape, but I guess none of us really believed him. He is so old, we thought he may be dreaming." Eliza shook her head. "If only Clara was here to see this day. Sammy and Clara went back years together. He helped her look for me and the other families she reunited."

"Your mother got her freedom before you, didn't she?"

"Yes, she did."

"Did you mind that? What I mean is did you…"

"Blame her? Not a bit. It wasn't possible for her to take me. She had to save herself. She had to take a chance just like you did, Wilma. Ain't nothing surer than that. Your daughter knows it just as much as I did."

"But what if it was much worse for her, you know, after she left? I heard how they treated runaways."

"Sounds like she needed to leave in a hurry anyway. Them soldiers weren't going to thank her for stopping them from beating up her man, were they? They just as likely were going to kill her after they had some fun with her." Eliza grabbed Wilma's hand. "You did the best thing any mama could do. I just wish I could help you find her is all. I ain't as good at finding people as Clara was."

"You have a lot of ex-slaves here. Maybe someone will know my baby," Wilma said almost praying.

"We got people from all over the place. There's a lot of trouble brewing down South," Eliza Jane said in answer. "Some say it's worse than ever before but I can't agree with that. I believe it's bad but at least we got our freedom."

"Do you still have trouble? I sensed some nasty minds yesterday when I took a walk in Denver."

"Ye, we got trouble. When is our people ever not got trouble. But we do all right so long as we stay away from the danger areas. Annie tole me you went for a walk. She done tole me what you say to the store keeper. You is real brave."

"You know Annie? She seems like a nice girl."

"She is. She's my sister's girl. You met her sister earlier."

Wilma had difficulty matching the girl who had greeted them earlier with the smiling Annie.

"Jane don't mean to be the way she is. She was as sweet as Annie until… Well, let's just say she met the wrong type of boys."

Wilma caught the look on Eliza's face and knew straight away what had happened to Jane.

"The poor girl. I guess the police weren't interested either?"

"No, they weren't. It's happened before and will happen again. We keep the younger girls at home as often as we can but they has to go out sometime. We try to have someone keep an eye on them. But it's difficult. A young black man will get into much more trouble for hitting a white boy regardless of what the white boy did. Some things have never changed."

Wilma thanked God for living in Clover Springs. While it wasn't perfect, at least none of the women she loved had to deal with being afraid to walk the streets. Not now that Dickinson and his kind had gone.

"Would you like to take a walk around? Maybe we can meet someone you knew from the old days?" Eliza Jane asked, standing up.

"Thank you but we would have to walk slow."

"Oh yes, your friend said you were ill."

"I was but I is much better now. So how many people live here?"

Eliza brought Wilma around to many different houses introducing her to various people. She didn't meet anyone she knew or knew of her and had to keep a lid on the disappointment filling her. Something could still happen.

Mrs. Grey finally returned with Sammy and his son trailing behind her.

"I hope you took it nice and slowly," Mrs. Grey greeted Wilma.

"I did. Stop bossing me around and get me a cup of coffee," Wilma replied making the people around them laugh.

"Yes, ma'am, immediately, ma'am," Mrs. Grey teased back.

"It is so lovely to see you two being so close despite everything," Eliza Jane commented wiping a tear of laughter from her eye.

"You have no idea how much I owe Wilma. She is the center of Clover Springs. Everyone loves her. She has about a hundred children who look on her as their nana."

Wilma blushed. "Mrs. Grey is exaggerating. I work at the town orphanage. We have rather a large number of children at the moment. It's difficult finding homes for them."

"It sure is. I assume they are white? Our orphanage is filled with black children. We have lots of people who would love to take them but they simply can't afford to. Jobs are difficult to come by but even when you have work, there is no guarantee the job will be there tomorrow."

"I've read about that in New York. A friend of ours has gone to see her old housekeeper. She said conditions are difficult for the poorer families."

"Everyone has their cross to bear," Eliza said before offering them a plate of cookies and some more coffee.

Sometime later, a child came in to announce their driver was back to collect them.

"Have you any plans for tomorrow?" Eliza Jane asked.

"No," Wilma replied on behalf of both of them."

"It's Sunday so we go to church. You are more than welcome to join us or you can meet us here afterwards. We tend to have a potluck lunch. There will be a lot of people who couldn't be here today due to it being a work day. You may meet someone who you knew from the old days."

"Church sounds wonderful. Wilma has become a very enthusiastic church goer," Mrs. Grey said, her teasing tone making people laugh once more.

Wilma poked her friend in the ribs. Sure she went to church but she would never describe herself as enthusiastic about it. She went to hear Father Molloy speak. Her faith was improving but there was something still holding back her belief.

"Come around ten and we can all walk to church together," Eliza Jane said.

They said their goodbyes and sat in contemplative silence on their journey back. When they returned to the hotel they asked for their meals in Mrs. Grey's room.

"I couldn't face the hypocrisy in the dining room again tonight, could you?"

Wilma shook her head, grateful her friend had suggested the idea. The last thing she needed now was for someone to treat her badly due to her color. She might just bite their head off.

CHAPTER 25

After breakfast in Wilma's room, they headed outside and took the same carriage they had used yesterday, over to Eliza Jane's house. They were early enough to walk to church with their new friend. Mrs. Grey had suggested it would be better to turn up with someone the rest of the congregation knew. Otherwise, they might be treated with suspicion.

The service was very different from what Wilma was used to. The vicar sang and clapped along with the congregation as everyone sang. The music was wonderful, raising the hairs on the back of her neck with its beauty. A quick glance at Lorena's face showed her friend was just as mesmerized.

The sermon was longer than Father Molloy usually delivered but Wilma didn't mind. The young preacher had a pleasant voice. She could listen to it for hours.

He didn't talk about hell or paying heavily for your sins. Instead, his sermon was all about a God who loved them. He asked for prayers for his friend Frederick Douglass. Wilma had heard of him, what black person hadn't? But until she had started reading his autobiography, she had not realized he believed not only in equal rights for all races but also for men and women. He supported the women's suffrage movement.

All too soon the service was over, and the congregation spilled out of the church. People stood around chatting while kids ran around playing reminding her of Rosa, John, and all the children back in Clover Springs.

"Mrs. Grey and Miss Wilma, this here be our preacher. He's a relation of Frederick Douglass but don't ask me to explain it. Once you go past first cousins, you got me confused," Eliza Jane exclaimed her smile making her eyes dance.

"Good morning. Thank you for a lovely sermon."

"That's high praise coming from Wilma, Reverend Douglass. She isn't known for her love of churches."

Wilma could have throttled Mrs. Grey until she realized Rev. Douglass was laughing.

"Eliza Jane told me you two were good friends. It's nice to see. Sets a good example for the rest of us," Reverend Douglass said. "Eliza Jane also told me why you came to Denver. I hope your quest is successful. Come with me and I will introduce you to some of our older ex-slaves. They may know something."

"Coming, Mrs. Grey?"

"No thank you, Wilma. I want to spend some time with Sammy and his family. See you later."

Wilma left Mrs. Grey in Eliza Jane's capable hands as she took the arm of the friendly young preacher.

"I heard you run an orphanage in Clover Springs. Do you find it difficult to find families for the children?"

"Sometimes. At the moment, we have a lot of children. Mrs. Grey jokes I have one hundred grandchildren. It's not quite that many, although it seems it at times," Wilma said before explaining about how Alicia and Father Molloy had rescued the orphans.

"Two children, Rosa and her brother John, break my heart. Such beautiful souls but their chances of being adopted are almost zero."

"Why?"

"Their father was black and their mother white. The black community in Boston didn't want them and we know what the white community is like. They have been living at the orphanage for over a year now, actually, make that nearly two years."

"I am sure they are well cared for."

"They are and we shower them with love but that

doesn't stop Rosa asking when her real parents will come and pick her. It's heartbreaking."

"There are so many things we could do if we had the funds to work with. Our people are generous but they have so little themselves." Reverend Douglass looked into the distance toward the area of Denver with the big houses and fancy buildings. "So many have so much and yet we have children who have few clothes and no shoes even in the depths of winter."

"How can you believe so strongly in a God that lets this happen?"

Reverend Douglass stopped walking and took Wilma's hands in his. Looking into her eyes, he said softly "God gave man free will. This is not God's doing but our own."

Wilma wasn't at all sure she agreed, but she didn't want to offend the young preacher.

"So where are these people you want me to meet?"

"Over here but first I would like to ask you a favor. I know we have just met and it is a little presumptuous but you have a warm heart. So does your white friend. Would you take one of our community back with you when you return to your town?"

"Jane?"

The look of astonishment on his face was funny. "Did Eliza mention this already?"

"No, Reverend Douglass but she told me what

happened to young Jane. We met her yesterday. Her heart is full of anger."

"Yes, it is and after what happened to her, few would blame the girl. But her mother worries she may get into more trouble. She has started taking big risks. She purposefully walks through areas we have been warned to avoid. It is as if she is baiting them on purpose."

"Or trying to prove what those animals did to her, hasn't destroyed her. But yes, whatever her reasons, she is putting herself in danger. I am more than happy to bring her to Clover Springs. She will be safe there. But will she want to come with us?"

"I do not know. I have yet to speak to her. But I sense she might be glad to move away. She thinks our people blame her for what happened." He took a large breath as if talking about Jane was difficult.

"Some probably do," Wilma agreed nodding her head. "In my experience, it is very easy for people who have never lived your life to cast judgement. She needs time away from everyone she knows in order to recover and come to terms with her ordeal. Maybe then she could come back."

"You are a very wise woman, Miss Wilma. I would like to come and visit your town for myself."

"Please do. Father Molloy, he's our Catholic priest,

would love to speak with you. He likes to meet with other preachers and exchange ideas."

"Will he try to convert me? I am not fit for the celibate life," he joked. "I quite like the idea of settling down and getting married."

Wilma followed his gaze to where it came to rest on Jane. Oh, the poor man. He was in love with a rape victim. She put her hand on his arm. "Mr. Douglass, if you can convince the girl to come with me, I promise to do everything I can to help her recover. I have some experience in this area, more than I ever hoped to have. I can tell you the girl you knew prior to the attack will never completely return. The attack and what she has suffered since will shape her personality, but with help, hopefully, she won't remain angry at the world."

Reverend Douglass squeezed Wilma's hand. "I am so grateful for what you are offering. I will try to convince her to go with you. Now let me introduce you to some people who may be able to help you."

The preacher led Wilma over to a group of older people who were sitting closest to the large fire someone had lit.

"We don't have an indoor space big enough to fit everyone, so if it is dry but cold, we light the fire so we can all sit together."

Wilma appreciated why. This was a real community with people of all ages gathered together. Some were chatting, some were playing instruments, others singing or cooking or both. The children were having fun, even the dogs and cats looked like they were smiling. For the first time in a very long time she had a flashback to what life had been like in her youth. A scene like this occupied her mind rather than the more savage moments she usually remembered. In her mind, she could see Granny tending the fire while everyone sat around chatting and having fun. Her ma and pa had been there, her pa's arms, which were as wide as a tree trunk, wrapped firmly around her ma's waist. She'd looked happy. Blinking her eyes rapidly removed the scene, it would only lead to tears and today was supposed to be a happy one.

* * *

"Ladies and gentlemen, this is Wilma. She's looking for her daughter, whom she last saw in eighteen sixty-four. I will leave you to chat. If I can do anything you know where to find me."

"Thank you, preacher, we will talk later about that other matter."

He shook her hand, gave her a warm smile and then left to speak to another group. Wilma suddenly felt like she was ten years old wondering if anyone would play with her.

"Come over here and rest a while. Get a bit of warmth into your bones. That preacher, he be a good one, but he can talk the hind legs off a horse."

Relieved, Wilma smiled at the lady and took a seat beside her.

"So tell us your story, Wilma, let's see can any of us help."

Wilma took a deep breath and told her story over again. She managed to get through it well enough, only the occasional tear escaped. The lady sitting beside her took her hand and held onto it tight as she stumbled over the last part.

"That's the last time I saws my baby girl. She ain't a baby no more, maybe she is dead. I just don't know."

"What was the name of her young friend?"

"Andrew but I don't know his surname. I don't think I ever did. It is like looking for one ear of corn in a whole corn field."

A few laughed at the analogy but one man kept staring at her, his eyes boring into her soul. She shifted, trying to escape his gaze but nothing she did worked.

"Zack, you cut that out. You is scaring her. That ain't nice."

Wilma expected an acknowledgment or even an

apology, but instead, the man called Zack got up and walked away.

"He don't say much. He got badly treated," the woman sitting beside her said, although her tone showed she was annoyed. "They caught him when he run away and brought him back. I won't give you the details of what happened next. He still carries the scars. But it's his heart that needs healing. He can't find his family neither."

"Maybe me being here brought back bad memories," Wilma said, although her head was telling her different. She had a feeling she'd met Zack before but she couldn't place where. It wasn't on the last plantation she lived on. Had it been somewhere since then?

She tried to dismiss Zack from her mind but she found it hard to do. There was something in his gaze calling to her. After a while, she decided to stretch her legs. She had told her story and for now that was all she could do. She went for a walk, telling herself she was looking for Lorena.

SHE WALKED DOWN to where Eliza Jane's house was but there was no sign of Lorena or any of Eliza Jane's family. She was about to turn back when she felt him staring at her again. She looked behind her and there he was. Not standing next to her but about twenty feet behind her.

"I knows you."

"You must be mistaken. I don't think we ever met," she denied, yet she knew he was right. But the memory wouldn't resurface. It was too scary.

"Yes, we did. A long time ago. Don't you remember?" His eyes bored into hers stirring up faint memories. The beating hot sun, thirst combined with fear, fifty other bodies of all ages crowded around her. A young man had given her a cup of water and got beaten severely for his trouble. That young man was…

"Yes, it's me. You was waiting for the auction block. You and your daughter, although I thought you was friends. She had paler skin."

Wilma continued to stare at him as the world turned black.

* * *

SHE CAME to lying on the sofa in Eliza Jane's home. Lorena was by her side, her face ashen with worry. The preacher was in the other chair and Eliza Jane was hovering. She tried to sit up but Mrs. Grey put her hand on her chest.

"Keep lying down for a few minutes. You had a nasty fall."

"Is he here?"

"Who?"

"Zack?"

"Is that the man she was talking to before she fainted?"

"Yes, Mrs. Grey, but we don't know where he went. Someone said he recognized Wilma."

"He did? But why has he gone? Doesn't he know she wants to speak to anyone who knew her in the past."

"Zack, find him. Please. He knows something," Wilma begged.

"Sammy will help me find him, but you got to promise me you will go back to the hotel and rest. Please, Wilma. If anything happens to you, Doc Erin and the other ladies will murder me."

"I will but please find him. Please."

Mrs. Grey left reluctantly. Wilma sat up although she didn't try to stand. The room was spinning.

"Reverend Douglass, thank you for coming but I is fine now. You go and enjoy your Sunday. I need to speak to Eliza Jane."

He looked as if he was going to argue but he didn't. He got up and left without saying a word.

"You got a way of managing him. Ain't never known him to stay silent before," Eliza Jane said.

"Are we alone?"

"Yes, Wilma, why? What's wrong. What's Zack done to make you faint?"

"Zack saved my life once, he took a terrible beating for it too. I had totally forgotten him. I owe him an apology," Wilma said before telling Eliza Jane all about the young man who had given her and Solace some water. They'd been in the cage for hours with nothing to eat or drink. The sun was burning down on them and their cage was situated in an area with no shade. Wilma had begged several people for water but they either ignored or jeered her or worse. Wilma had to take a couple of deep breaths at that point in her story. She could feel the terror as clear as it had been that day. Her master had decided to sell her and Solace with a group of other slaves from his plantation. She'd been terrified they'd be separated. Solace was only about ten years old. She was in high demand due to her beauty and paler skin. Wilma, being twenty-five or six at that time, was also deemed valuable due to her beauty. She prayed the buyer would select both of them. That way she would have a chance to protect Solace from the brutality of the world they lived in. Just as she thought Solace would faint from thirst, someone gave her hope and belief in humanity.

A man not much older than she was, he said he was a free man, came forward and gave her a cup of water. That is all he did and for that he was abused and beaten. They didn't believe he was a free man. Made up some story about his papers being invalid. He was thrown into the cage with them.

"I ruined his life, Eliza Jane. If he had kept on going, he would never have been on that auction block."

"You didn't do nothing. The white men did it, not you. Zack did what he did because he can't bear to see suffering. He still can't. He was the first man Jane would let touch her. He gave her a hug. He's still the only one she will talk to. Properly I mean."

"But the woman said he suffered very badly."

Eliza Jane looked out the window for a few seconds. Then she looked at Wilma face to face. "It's true. He did. He ran away but the slave catchers caught him. Brought him back to our master. He was furious. Everyone was running and he wanted to make an example of someone. That person was Zack," Eliza Jane shuddered. "I can't ever tell you what they did. We thought he would die. But he fought back and he's been fighting since. He ran again but next time he didn't come back. I was sure he'd been killed."

"So he was on the same plantation as you?"

"Yes. Until he ran. Mama found him a few years back. He was looking for his family. They'd been free too. His previous master had given the whole family their freedom after he went to one of Fredrick

Douglass's talks. Zack was only a boy then but he grew up free. His papers were just fine. But they didn't save him."

"What happened to his family?"

"Nobody knows. He never found his parents. He has an ex-wife. I don't know whether he has children."

Wilma sat clenching her dress in her hands. She was the reason the poor man had lost everything. Just to give her a drink of water.

"Eliza Jane, can you ask Jane to find him for me? Please. Tell him I just want to thank him for what he done for me?"

"I will. Now you rest. Please. You got a bad shock."

"I will but before I do, do you know what your preacher asked me to do?"

Eliza Jane nodded.

"You agree it is for the best?"

"Yes, Wilma, I do. She's never going to get well here. Too many memories."

"Are you going to ask her, or will I?"

"Could you ask her, Wilma? She won't talk to me. Accuses me of favoring Annie. I love them both as if they were my own. It kills me to think of her hurting so much."

This time it was Wilma's turn to hug Eliza Jane and offer what little comfort she could.

CHAPTER 26

Wilma waited in Eliza Jane's home for Jane to come in. Eliza had provided coffee and cookies but Wilma wasn't in the mood for eating. She thought about what she could offer the girl. How could she make her trust her? Could she convince her to give Clover Springs a chance?

The door opened and Jane came in, her face screwed up in anger. Resentment leaked from every pore of her body. Wilma pretended not to notice.

"Jane, come and sit with me. I think I have spoken to everyone in Eliza Jane's extended family but you."

"I don't want to talk."

"All right then, why don't you sit and I'll talk."

Jane couldn't really do anything but sit down. Wilma had counted on her being a well brought up young woman and disrespecting your elders wasn't something she would be accustomed to doing. Wilma wasn't above using Jane's upbringing to her advantage.

"I heard some—"

"I know what you is going to say. It was all my fault. I shouldn't have been there. I must have…"

Wilma laid a gentle hand on the girl's arm stopping her mid tirade.

"Actually, I wasn't going to say any of those things. I don't know exactly what happened to you, Jane, but one thing I know is you did nothing wrong." Wilma put her finger under Jane's chin and gently forced the young woman to meet her eyes. "Did you hear me? Nothin' you did or didn't do made those boys behave the way they did. There is evil in this world. You got caught up in that. I is very sorry that happen to you."

Wilma watched the emotions play out on the young woman's face. Now she was looking at her closely she could see the resemblance to her sister, Annie. If Jane smiled, she would look just like her sibling and a little like her aunt.

"I knows this too. You is a strong woman. You come from a line of strong women. Your grandma would be proud of you."

"You don't know anythin'."

"Yes, I do, dear. I more than most know exactly how you feel."

Jane's eyes widened.

"Years ago, things like that happened quite a lot. How do you think there are so many ex-slaves that look more white than black? You think our kind had love affairs with the masters?"

Jane shook her head.

"No, we was their property to do what they liked with. They could keep us, sell us, share us... All they cared about was their feelings, their happiness." Wilma stopped. She didn't want to burden the girl with the whole sorry tale of what had likely happened to her mother, grandmother, and other females in her family. "I would love you to come back with me to Clover Springs."

"I ain't going nowhere. I ain't going to run and look like a coward."

"Well, that is your choice as you are free now. Freedom comes with a price. Now we is responsible for the choices we make. Back in Clover Springs, we have a few people who made bad decisions in their lives but they put it behind them and live wonderful lives now. It's different there. Sure there are some people who see color first and the person last but that is going to happen everywhere. But nobody treats me badly. We have an Indian as a deputy sheriff and you can bet your last dollar, he doesn't put up with any nonsense."

"Can you really go where you want?" Jane's eyes were brighter than before.

"Well yes, within reason."

"See it's the same as here then."

The sullenness was back but Wilma tried to remain patient. "Well, I don't think your aunt would allow you to go into a saloon. Would she?"

Jane shook her head.

"That's the same in Clover Springs. No self-respecting woman would go into the saloon, and if you did make that mistake, Gary would see you home. He'd tell me, too, and I would tan your backside."

Jane giggled at the ferocious look on Wilma's face.

"Why don't you come see it for yourself? What you got to lose?"

"Nothin'."

"Well then? Come home with me and stay for a little while. You don't have to stay forever. After you got your head straight you can decide what you want to do."

Jane didn't look convinced but Wilma thought she saw a spark of interest in her eyes. She decided to assume Jane would say yes.

"You will have to work though. Nobody lives in my house and lies around all day. We got plenty of laundry and cooking and minding children to be doing."

"I like working with children, Miss Wilma. They don't care whether you are black or white."

"Most of them don't but some pick up bad habits from their parents. But that's a discussion for another day. Why don't you find your aunt and tell her you are coming home with me?"

"Miss Wilma, why are you helping me like this? Is it because of your daughter?"

"A little but its more to do with your preacher asking me to do it. He is a very nice young man who adores you," Wilma said gently watching Jane's face closely.

"Used to adore me. He won't touch me now," Jane said angrily.

"Sweetheart, with that look on your face all the time, I am not sure there is a man alive brave enough to do that."

Jane giggled just as her aunt walked through the door.

"Jane, you're laughing. Oh my goodness what a beautiful sound." Before Jane could say anything, she was swept into a big hug. Her eyes met Wilma's over her aunt's shoulder. Wilma gave her a thumbs-up just as she would to Rosa when the little girl made progress with something. Jane was a brave girl, the road ahead wasn't going to be easy, but she would recover. Wilma was confident of that. Almost as sure of the fact that Jane's arrival in town would upset Ma Kelley and Mrs. Shaw not to mention Charlie Staunton.

CHAPTER 27

"Are you ready to go home, Wilma? Or do you want to wait to see if Zack turns up?"

"No, I need to go home. I don't like it here. I don't feel safe," Wilma admitted despite hating the fact she was weak.

"I can see why. There is a simmering discontent under the surface as if someone is waiting for something to happen. Maybe that's in all big cities but I can't wait to get home. At least in Clover Springs, we know who the villains are."

"Yes, aren't they going to be really upset when they see who we bring home with us?"

Mrs. Grey kept a straight face as she said, "I have no idea what you mean, Miss Wilma."

Both burst out laughing. "I feel like a school girl, but can you make sure I am there to see their faces when they first hear about Jane? We should say the whole of Eliza Jane's community is coming to live in Clover Springs. Would that be enough to get rid of Mrs. Shaw once and for all?"

Wilma couldn't reply to Mrs. Grey as she was still laughing. They were acting like little children but who cared. Nobody could see them. They weren't harming anyone.

"Just in case I forget to say it, thank you for bringing me here. You are the truest friend." Wilma took Lorena's hand in hers and kissed it, the tears filling up her eyes.

"I feel so bad though. I got more out of coming here. I got to meet Sammy and his family. I got to share my memories of my precious David. While you got to pick up another waif."

"I am glad we can help Jane but I got far more than that, Lorena Grey. I got my belief in human nature back. There is good and bad in every race. That will never change but I can focus on the good now. Maybe I will never find my daughter but I can help those who need me. That's enough for me."

Lorena Grey surprised herself as much as Wilma by dragging her into a hug.

"I love you, Miss Wilma. I think after speaking to Sammy, I can finally let David go. I didn't let him down, did I? I finally saw the light even if it took me some time."

"I never knew what you was like before Miss Ellen worked her magic on you. But I got to say, some of the stories I've been told about your early years in Clover Springs, I sure is glad I didn't end up there earlier."

Although Wilma was teasing, Lorena looked at her sadly. "Maybe if you had, my friend, I would have seen the light earlier. I have a daughter who is alive and well and I know where she lives but she won't see me. Not that I blame her," Lorena said.

"We could call to see her on the way back if she doesn't live too far away?"

"Absolutely not, Wilma, I can't stand the woman. She is a replica of me when I was younger. No, I am happy to draw a line under that part of my life."

"Does that mean you are ready to move on?"

"To what?" Lorena said suspiciously.

"I happen to know a certain man is quite eager to share your fireplace," Wilma teased.

Despite her friend's denials she had a feeling Sheriff Willis wouldn't have to do much convincing.

* * *

THE TRAIN JOURNEY back passed very quickly as they showed Jane the sights. The poor girl was so nervous she could barely speak. Both Wilma and Mrs. Grey tried to reassure her everything would be fine but their assurances fell on deaf ears.

When they arrived, they were surprised to see Father Molloy waiting at the station for them. At least Wilma was.

"You sent a telegram to say we were coming home?" she accused Mrs. Grey.

"I thought you would appreciate a warm welcome."

"It's good to be home." Wilma sighed as the train pulled in. It had barely stopped and she was out of the car.

"That woman thinks she is still a twenty-year-old," Mrs. Grey muttered to Jane but Jane didn't respond. She was too busy taking in her new surroundings.

"Father Molloy, this is a special friend of mine. Jane Harris, I would like you to meet Father Molloy. He is the priest we spoke about."

"I hope you said nice things about me, Wilma. If she didn't, Miss Harris, she was telling lies." Father Molloy held out his hand smiling.

Jane stared at his hand and then at his face. His smile faltered a little but Wilma could see the pity he had for Jane.

"Jane, this is one of my dearest friends. Be nice," Wilma muttered under her breath.

Jane shook the priest's hand reluctantly before dropping back to walk behind them.

"Another waif?" Father Molloy whispered to Wilma.

"Her aunt is the lady we went to see. We have a story to tell you, Father Molloy, but first, I is dying for a decent cup of tea."

"Tea?"

"Yes. If I have another cup of coffee I will burst. I want me some of Miss Ellen's hot tea with milk in it. Then I knows I am home."

'You are home and we have missed you dearly. Both of you." Father Molloy was quick to include Mrs. Grey. Wilma noted the look of happiness on her friend's face. The trip had helped to remove some of her pain and therefore gruffness. Clover Springs was in for a nice surprise.

"So tell us all the news. How are Rosa, John, and the rest of my young'uns'? Are Doc Erin and Alicia enjoying New York? Has Ma Kelley moved away?"

Father Molloy let out a belly laugh startling Jane.

"Wilma, please never change. The young'uns are fine, Mrs. Kelley and her friends are all still in residence," Father Molloy said shrugging his shoulders.

"As of today, there is still no word from Doc Erin and Alicia so I imagine they are having too much fun."

THEY ENTERED the orphanage where they were inundated by the children welcoming Wilma home. It took Wilma a few minutes to get them all under control.

"Children, we have a new guest come to stay with us for a while. Her name is Jane and her aunt is a friend of mine. Please say hello."

"Hello, Jane," the children chorused.

Rosa moved closer to Jane and pulled at her dress to get her attention.

"We ain't got a lot of room at the moment but you can have my bed, and I will sleep on the floor here with my friends."

Jane looked so terrified Wilma quickly intervened.

"Rosa, you know you is happy with Miss Ellen and Samuel and John. Jane is goin' to share my room for a while until we see how she gets on. When she is ready, she may stay in the Haven with Doc Erin."

"I hope you like it here. We do. I was born somewhere else but I love living here," Rosa explained to Jane. Jane didn't have to answer as Rosa continued to tell her all about living in Clover Springs and about school.

"We got a new teacher. Are you going to go to school too?"

"Jane is a little old to be going to school but she might go and say hello to your new teacher, but now, could you show her my room so she can put her things away?"

"Yes, Miss Wilma. Come this way Jane."

Rosa held onto Jane's hand so firmly the girl had no choice but to follow. When she left, Wilma checked to see she was out of earshot and quickly explained the situation to Ellen, Samuel, and Father Molloy.

"Samuel, she won't say a word to you. At least not initially. She didn't trust no man apart from one back in Denver."

"I don't blame her. I would like to get my hands on those…"

"Samuel Higgins, I am still present as are the ladies."

Wilma had to hide her smile as Samuel looked like a child being told off but she appreciated his sentiments. She knew he and Little Beaver would help her restore Jane's faith in men. But they would have to take things very slowly.

"What else have I been missing?" Wilma said, drinking a cup of tea.

"Charlie Staunton wants to marry the new teacher. But he's not the only one."

"Well, no matter who the alternative is, he has to be better than Staunton. He should marry Ma Kelley," Wilma replied.

"Murph was interested, for a while."

"Oh, the poor girl, is she still here? She is goin' to think this town is full of horrible men."

"Murph is all right once he keeps his political views under his hat. I think he has competition anyway. Gary Barrett seems to have taken a real interest in Miss Templeton."

"He is a nice man. Does she like him?"

'Hard to know what she thinks of anyone to be honest. She is so British."

"Father Molloy," Wilma and Mrs. Grey chorused.

"I don't mean it in a bad way, but she has been brought up to conceal her feelings. Honestly, I think if someone insulted her, she would thank them politely."

"How is she getting on with the children?"

"She has put Master Shaw in his place a couple of times, but I sense she needs to be a little braver. Again she is too…"

"Polite," the ladies said this time, laughing at the expression on the priest's face.

"I feel bad for her actually. With you and Doc Erin away, Emer Shipley was busy with the clinic, Katie with the store, and Laura and Ellen are both still recovering. There was nobody for her to talk to."

"You could have taken her out to see Mary."

"Mary Ryan Sullivan is the kindest soul that ever walked the earth but she'd question a tree till it answered her. The last thing Miss Templeton needs now is an inquisition."

Wilma exchanged a look with Mrs. Grey. Just what did the priest know about the new teacher that he was afraid would be shared with the rest of the community?

"Ladies, I am so glad to have you both back safe and sound. I must be getting back to work. I haven't got the sermon written for Sunday. I thought it was Reverend Timmons' turn but he insists it is mine."

Wilma grinned. Reverend Timmons knew the people preferred to listen to Father Molloy so he often asked him to speak instead.

* * *

LATER THAT NIGHT, when she was almost asleep Wilma heard Jane sobbing. She'd thought the girl was fast asleep when she came into the room. She moved quickly to her side.

"Come on, let it all out, Jane sweetie. You will feel better."

"I miss my aunt and my sister and most of all

Reverend Douglass. Will he forget me now I have moved away?"

"That's one thing that definitely won't happen. He loves you just as much as he ever did, perhaps even more. Don't forget it was his idea for you to come and stay with us. Someday soon, when you is feelin' better, you must invite him to come and see what Clover Springs is like. You'll see, Jane, this place has the power to change lives. I know you don't think you will ever feel the same again, and you are probably right. But you will have the strength to put your ordeal behind you and make a good life for yourself, and for Reverend Douglass if that is your desire."

Wilma cuddled Jane until she fell asleep and only then did she climb into her own bed. It was lovely to be home, but exhausted as she was, she couldn't sleep. Somewhere out there her daughter could still be alive. Would she ever see her again?

CHAPTER 28

The next morning, Wilma got up early despite being tired. She wanted to see the children off to school, especially Rosa.

"Mornin', Wilma, I is so glad you is home."

"Me too, darlin'. So how are you gettin' on at school? Do you like your new teacher? Is she nice?"

"She is but she says she is really worried about my…what did she call it? Grammar? She says I need to speak proper but I do. Don't I? You understand me. She won't answer me if I ask her a question and use ain't."

Wilma looked away so the child wouldn't see she was amused. She didn't want Rosa thinking she was laughing at her.

"I think Miss Templeton is only trying to make you speak like a lady."

"But you use ain't and ole and stuff like that all the time. And you is a lady."

"You are a lady," Wilma corrected softly. "I am not like your Miss Templeton. I ain't never, I mean I never went to school."

"Was your mama really nice? She must be to let you off from school"

Wilma loved Rosa's innocence but the child needed to know where her ancestors came from.

"No, sweetie, it wasn't my mama's wish for me not to go to school. I had to go to work like all the other children where I lived."

"Work? Not just chores?"

"No, darling, it was real work not chores. Have you learned about the slaves yet?"

"No, but that dumb old Bertram Shaw keeps saying I is one. Is it a bad name?"

"It is but it wasn't our fault. See, at one time in some places in America, most black people were slaves. People like me had to work on big plantations from a very young age. Our masters weren't interested in no book learning. They says we never need it. But they was wrong. Book learning is very important, Rosa. Only with education can you truly be free."

"Was I an ex-slave?"

"No, Abraham Lincoln, may God bless his soul,

abolished slavery a long time ago. You were born free just as free as Bertram Shaw."

"I is going to ask Miss Templeton to tell us about slavery. We should all know about it. Thank you, Wilma." Rosa kissed Wilma on the cheek before finishing off her breakfast and running to find her friends.

Wilma sat there rubbing her cheek wishing, as she so often did, Rosa was her real grandchild.

CHAPTER 29

"Miss Eleanor, what do you know about being a slave?"

Rosa stood up, her big brown eyes sparkling with innocence. She couldn't possibly mean anything by her question, could she? But why ask her? Why not Ellen or Laura?

"Not a lot, Rosa. Just what I read in the papers. It's abolished now, though, so you don't need to worry about it."

"Yeah, Miss Wilma tole me it's gone but why was it allowed? You don't think it's right for people to own other people, do you?"

"No, Rosa, I don't think it's right at all. I don't know why it first started. I have some theories but you are too young to understand them."

"Do you have slaves in England?"

"No, Bertram, we don't." Eleanor tried to keep her tone civil but it was very difficult with Bertram. She usually could find redeeming qualities in most people but with this child, she was struggling.

"If I asked someone Irish would they agree with you?"

She clenched her fists, her nails digging into the palms of her hands.

"Yes, of course, they would. There is, and never was, slavery in Ireland. I believe the Irish have been treated badly on countless occasions but this is not a subject on our curriculum."

"Why? Because you feel bad for being mean to Irish people?"

"That's enough, Bertram," she said firmly. She wasn't in the mood for his bad behavior. Rosa's question had shaken her more than she liked. What had life been like for her mother, grandparents, and extended family. She knew it hadn't been pleasant.

"I was just saying..."

"I said enough. Go stand in the corner. Now."

Bertram got up grumbling but he went to stand in the corner. The other students peered at their slates or books, anywhere but at her face.

Rosa put her hand up again.

"Yes, Rosa."

"Miss Eleanor, will it happen again? Will people

put me back in slavery?"

The terrified look on the child's face made Eleanor feel ill.

"No, Rosa, nobody will let that happen to you. Now why don't you show the class how well you can read?"

"I only started reading, Miss Eleanor."

"I know but Miss Laura said you have been working very hard."

Rosa's smile lit up the whole room. "I has been. I promise."

Although tempted to correct her grammar, Eleanor didn't. This sweet child needed encouragement to reach her potential. Eleanor resolved to ask Rosa's friend Wilma to teach her more about slavery. She knew very little. It wasn't a subject much discussed back in Britain.

* * *

THE CHILDREN CAME BACK in from recess but a quick count showed Rosa was missing.

"Laura, Rosa didn't come back in. Has she gone home?"

"No, the children aren't allowed go home unless they get permission from one of us. Is she in the outhouse?"

"No, miss, 'cause I was just there."

"Thanks, Billy," Laura answered before asking Eleanor to go outside and check.

Eleanor went outside, the outhouse was empty, and there was no sign of the little girl. She stood looking for a few seconds. Gary Barrett came over to her.

"Something wrong?"

"One of the children didn't come back after recess."

"Who?"

"Rosa."

"I'll help you look. She may have gone over to those trees. Kids are always climbing them."

Eleanor picked up her skirt and followed Gary, gingerly walking through the higher grass. Didn't snakes hide in grass? But they went into hibernation, didn't they? She racked her brain trying to remember. She could deal with anything, but snakes of any shape, size, poisonous or not, scared her to pieces.

"Isn't that Rosa up above?" Gary pointed to a little girl sitting on the branch of a tree. "Shall I bring her over to you? I don't fancy your chances of getting over those branches in that skirt."

"Yes, please. Thank you."

Eleanor watched as Gary went over to Rosa. He bent down and spoke to her. She looked back in Eleanor's direction. The poor child had been crying. Who had upset her?

"Rosa is a bit upset. I said you would be able to help her."

"Of course I can, darling. You tell me what's wrong."

"Someone is going to come and take me and make me a slave again."

"Nobody will do that, Rosa. Slavery ended years ago."

"Well, Bertram said I don't have a real ma and pa. I never will because I ain't black or white so nobody wants me. So they get people like me to do the work slaves used to do. Because nobody cares about us." The child's sobs made Eleanor want to cry. After she boxed Bertram's ears. Before she could say anything, Gary bent down to Rosa's level.

"Listen to me, little one. Any person who got to adopt a sweet, kind, wonderful girl like you would be very lucky. You can't just have anyone as a parent. You have to wait for someone really special to come along."

"That's what Miss Wilma says, but I thought she was trying to make me feel better."

"Miss Wilma knows it is always best to tell the truth, doesn't she?" Gary asked.

Rosa nodded, her thumb in her mouth but her gaze fixed on Gary's face.

"I know you want to be part of a family but for now, you got a lot to be happy about. You got Miss

Wilma and Miss Ellen and Mr. Samuel and all the other children in the orphanage. You got friends in Clover Springs and most of all you have your big brother, who always looks out for you. That's more than a lot of girls have."

"All girls have a big brother, don't they Miss Eleanor?"

"No, Rosa, they don't. Some people don't have any siblings, I mean brothers or sisters. Like me."

"And me," Gary added.

"Oh. I is lucky," Rosa said before sticking her thumb back into her mouth.

"You are very lucky. Now will you come back to school with me?"

"Yes, Miss Eleanor. Am I in trouble?"

"A little bit because we were worried about you and if Mr. Barrett hadn't come along, I think I would have spent a long time looking for you," Eleanor said using her teacher's voice. At the look on the child's face, she mellowed. "But I think you have been punished enough so let's forget about it." She smiled at the child to show her she wasn't angry.

"One thing though, Rosa, next time Bertram Shaw says anything to upset you, you tell him to come see me. I got plenty to say to him," Gary said.

"Thank you, Mr. Barrett, but I shall deal with Master Shaw," Eleanor corrected him firmly.

His ears pinked but he didn't disagree with her.

"Come along, Rosa, let's get back inside," Eleanor said softly taking the little girl's hand

"Thank you, Mr. Barrett, for coming to save me. I hope the pa who adopts me will be just like you."

Rosa let Eleanor's hand go and ran back to the school house leaving Eleanor alone with a stunned looking Gary.

"She's such a sweet little thing, isn't she?" Eleanor stated the obvious more to break the silence than anything else.

"She sure is. A pa would be lucky to have her as his daughter."

The look of longing in his eyes almost took her breath away. Then it was gone. She wished she could take his hand or something but she was outside the school. Goodness knows who was watching.

"Thank you for your help, Mr. Barrett." Her voice caught on his surname but she couldn't call him Gary.

"No need for thanks. I would do almost anything for that little girl. She is such a beauty."

She stood staring at him as he walked away. Was he being honest? Could he see past Rosa's color to the child inside? If he could, then maybe he could accept her. Should she share her secret? What if she was wrong?

CHAPTER 30

"Children, I have asked Miss Wilma to come and talk to you about slavery. I know some of you have become very curious about this sorrowful period in our past. I don't think there is anyone better to educate us than someone who lived through it," Ellen said addressing the class.

Eleanor wanted to run and hide somewhere. Ellen had obviously talked to Wilma because she hadn't had a chance. She would have preferred to speak to Wilma in private. She wasn't ready emotionally to hear Wilma describe what it might have been like for her mother and other relations. But she couldn't move. To do so would be disrespectful and may also cause suspicion. She had no choice but to listen.

"Please don't anyone interrupt. If you have a question, write it down on your slate and you can ask at the end," Ellen added.

"I can't write too well, Miss Ellen," one of the younger children protested.

"That's okay, you can whisper it to me and I will remember for you."

The child beamed at Ellen who took a seat beside her.

* * *

Eleanor watched Wilma walk up to the front of the class. She had a real sense of dignity about her person but in a gentle rather than aggressive way. She started by smiling at the children.

"Most of you know I don't speak proper. I ain't ever had the chance to learn like you have. Yesterday, my little petal, Rosa, asked me was that because my ma loved me enough to keep me home all day."

The children giggled.

"But the truth is my ma didn't have a choice. I had to go and work. Just like she did. Just like everyone in the slave quarters did."

"But you were just a child like us," John said.

"Children, what did I say? Please listen quietly," Ellen reminded the class.

"Yes, I was just a child but children can be good

cotton pickers. Anyways, we didn't have a choice. We did whatever the master tole us to do." Wilma looked around the room. "The master was in charge of everything. What we wore, what we ate, how we spent our days, whether we could have a preacher, get married, stay together. The only thing that was free were our thoughts. Most slaves thought about freedom but few were brave enough to run away."

"Why? I'd run away rather than let anyone keep me prisoner. But then nobody would 'cause I am white."

"Bertram, show some respect to your elders. The people couldn't run away as the master would punish not only them but their family members who stayed behind. If your ma was going to be hurt because you ran away, would you go?" Ellen asked.

"Yup."

Some of the children laughed but most gave Bertram a dirty look. When he realized his antics were not appreciated, it only made him worse.

"School is for learning about math and English. We don't need to listen to no sob stories. They aren't true anyway. They is only made up. My ma says that you got nothing more than you deserved and if she had her way, you wouldn't be allowed to live among decent people."

"Of all the horrible things I have ever heard, your outburst ranks high on that list. Your mother should be made to come here and listen to what this good lady is saying. The truth will always come out and nobody can hide it. You are a despicable young man but it sounds like your ma is even worse. How dare you disrespect someone who has lived with the horror of being enslaved."

Silence greeted her outburst. She bit her lip in horror at what she had said. She meant every word but it was pointless aiming her anger at a young boy.

"Thank you for your kindness, Miss Eleanor, but perhaps you should take the rest of the day off. I can see this is quite distressing for you," Ellen said kindly but her eyes held a warning telling Eleanor to leave.

Eleanor understood why. She had lashed out at a child. That was never acceptable behavior.

"Why do you care? You is white. It's never going to happen to you." Bertram looked around the class. "Nobody is going to put white people into slavery. We are the masters. If you don't like that…"

"Bertram Shaw, go home now. I will call later to see your mother. Get out of this classroom immediately." Ellen's tone showed how annoyed she was.

"Make me."

"Are you always this disrespectful young man?" Father Molloy's voice boomed over the classroom. "I do not know what has been going on here, but judging by the number of upset faces, I can only imagine you are up to your old tricks. Get out of this classroom now, and I will take you to see your mother."

"That ain't fair. You wasn't here to hear her lies."

"The only person not telling the truth is you, Master Shaw. Wilma has been a dear friend of mine for many years. I will not stand by and see you or anyone else treat her so badly. Now get out."

The priest shouting was such an unusual event Bertram did what he was told. Rosa started to cry along with some other young children. Eleanor knew she should stay and help but she couldn't. She was too distressed as well. She pushed past the children and ran outside.

CHAPTER 31

Sometime later, Eleanor heard someone knocking at the door to the boarding house. Wiping her eyes, she was tempted to ignore it. She couldn't do anything about the redness of her face. One look and they would know she'd been weeping.

The knocking continued as Father Molloy called out her name.

She went downstairs quickly and opened the door, admitting Father Molloy and Wilma. She immediately looked at the woman and saw her eyes filled with questions and concern. What had Father Molloy told her?

"Wilma insisted on coming with me to check on you. She thought you might need a woman's ear. And she brought cookies."

She had to invite them in for coffee. To do otherwise would be extremely rude.

"Thank you very much for coming. I wasn't expecting anyone. Martha Sullivan isn't here but I can make some coffee."

"I can make the coffee, you find a plate for these and some cups." Wilma thrust the basket into her hand and headed toward the kitchen. She obviously knew her way around. Father Molloy gave her a gentle smile before following Wilma and leaving her standing in the hall. Taking a deep breath, she hoped she had the strength to explain her reaction to Bertram Shaw in a believable fashion.

Soon they were all seated enjoying a lovely cup of coffee and cookies which tasted as good as they smelled.

"I am sorry I was ill when you first came to Clover Springs, Miss Templeton. With my subsequent trip to Denver, I have been neglectful of my duties."

Eleanor raised an eyebrow not understanding what Wilma had to do with a new school teacher.

"Wilma usually makes it a point to get to know all newcomers to Clover Springs," Father Molloy elaborated.

"Don't apologize. Everyone has been lovely to me. It's a very nice town."

"It is but it would be nicer if some who lived here,

moved elsewhere," Wilma retorted.

Eleanor hid a smile as Father Molloy gently reprimanded Wilma.

"Now, Wilma, don't start. Miss Templeton isn't interested in gossip."

Eleanor exchanged a quick look with Wilma and then had to look down at her lap for fear of laughing. Like most women, she enjoyed a chat about the people in any town. Not in a nasty way but as a means of getting to know people. But she wasn't about to dim Father Molloy's high opinion of her.

"I am very sorry for not staying around today after Bertram's outburst. I behaved badly and I will apologize to the class tomorrow."

"You absolutely will not. What you said had to be said. Pity you didn't have his mother there too. I have no idea how to change that woman's mind," Father Molloy said, defeat evident in his tone.

"Some people is never going to listen to nobody. They believe they is better because their skin is white. It's the same everywhere. I guess it's that way in England too isn't it, Miss Templeton?"

"Please call me Eleanor," Eleanor said in a bid to buy herself some time to answer the question properly. She saw the speculative light in Father Molloy's eyes. He was waiting for her to admit the truth but she wasn't quite ready to do that yet.

"We don't have as much of a problem as you seem to have here simply because there aren't that many non-white people," Eleanor hedged catching the gleam in the priest's eyes. "There is a rigid class system which is something similar. There are those who condemn anyone who is poor as being lazy or a drinker or a woman of loose morals. From what I have seen, it is very easy to make disparaging comments about those less well-off than yourself. Most of my friends were born into wealth so they wouldn't know how to do a day's work if it was needed." Eleanor blushed as she admitted, "Gary Barret had to save this house from being burnt down. I tried to cook and well, let's just say, it didn't go very well."

"Oh, Martha is out of town, isn't she?"

"She left again last night. The first time she had to go because the children weren't well but now her daughter Elizabeth is sick. It must be a challenge to be sick and pregnant never mind have young children to mind too."

"You poor girl trying to cook for yourself in a strange kitchen. You should come to the orphanage for your meals at least until Martha comes back. Isn't that right, Wilma?"

"Yes, of course, it is fine for you to invite people to my kitchen for me to cook for? Don't I have enough to do without inviting every waif and stray to dinner?"

Wilma protested but she winked at Eleanor over the priest's head to show her she was joking.

"Wilma, I told you we had to be nice to Miss Templeton."

"Why? Looks like she is capable of looking after herself. That's true, ain't it?"

"Father Molloy, I think Wilma is teasing you. I would love to come to dinner some days if that was all right. I am getting fed up of bacon and eggs which is about all I could master."

"That's settled then. You will have to excuse me ladies, I have a sermon to write and a visit with Mrs. Shaw."

"Good luck with that, Father. I don't envy you not one little bit."

Father Molloy ignored Wilma. "Miss Templeton, would you like to come and see Mrs. Shaw with me?"

"I don't think so, Father, I am so annoyed I could say anything and make the situation worse."

"Yes, well, maybe that wouldn't be a good idea. I will take my leave. Good evening, ladies."

Eleanor showed Father Molloy to the door as Wilma sat firmly in her seat. Eleanor tried to calm her beating heart as she returned to the kitchen to talk to Wilma. She sensed the woman wasn't just staying on for some chit chat.

CHAPTER 32

Wilma waited until the new teacher came back from showing Father Molloy out. She sensed there was something troubling the young girl and she wanted to help if she could. She did feel bad for not being around when she'd first arrived in town. Even if Eleanor didn't know about how she had berated Father Molloy for bringing yet another needy person to her door, her unkindness still made her feel guilty.

"Take a seat please, Miss Templeton. I don't need any more coffee. I have to rest on doctor's orders. Have you met our Doc Erin yet?"

"Only briefly. She was heading to New York with another lady and her family."

"Miss Alicia. She will be a good friend to you when

she gets back. She understands what it is like to come from a rich family and settle here in Clover Springs."

"I like living here. I meant it when I said the people were kind."

"They are. But you are hiding something from us, aren't you? Father Molloy told me your father died and then your family asked you to leave. Can you tell me why?"

She saw Eleanor was taken aback by her directness. She leaned over to take the girl's hand in hers. "I is not trying to pry in your business and I certainly wouldn't say anything to nobody. I just get the feelin' you is struggling with something. You can't shock me. I just about heard everything there is to hear."

She stroked Eleanor's hand gently as she saw the disbelief in the girl's eyes.

"I used to work in a house of ill repute. Have you been told that? Never mind answering, your look of shock speaks volumes." Wilma laughed. "It's true."

"You did? You have lived an interesting life."

Eleanor's choice of words made Wilma smile. She had been well brought up. Only educated people would use interesting to describe living in a brothel.

"If you only knew. We all got secrets, girl, some prettier than others. But I learned something over my last week in Denver. You can't keep them to yourself.

They got a way of twisting up your insides so you turn to jelly."

"I guess you're right but...well, the last time someone found out my secret, I lost my home and family overnight. I don't think I could bear that to happen again." Eleanor's voice caught as she attempted to hide her distress.

Wilma pulled her into her arms and let her cry on her shoulder. God love her, she could only be about twenty and yet she was carrying the world on her shoulders.

"You listen to me and you listen good. You don't need to tell me nothing. Or you can tell me everything. Either way, I am your friend and that is never going to change."

Eleanor hiccupped before reaching for a hanky.

"The people of Clover Springs, most of them, will behave just like I do. Not that I am suggesting for a minute you tell everyone. That's none of their business. But you can trust people like Martha Sullivan and any of her family, Mrs. Grey—she isn't half as scary as she tries to make out. My darling Laura is another good soul. Oh, there are so many to mention." Wilma pushed the chair back as she stood up. "Don't take too long though. Although I applaud everything you said today to Bertram, and I am very grateful for your support, fact is, he is a child and he is repeating the rubbish his mother spouts. If you want to change him, you got to start with her."

"I know I behaved badly, lashing out at the child like that. I must apologize tomorrow."

"You will do no such thing," Wilma said vehemently. "Normally, I am in favor of an adult admitting a mistake. It shows children we are human too. But in this case, you would be admitting a weakness. Bertram Shaw will be a little intimidated by you for a while. That is a good thing."

"Thank you, Wilma, when I feel ready to talk, I will, but for the moment, I need time to work through it myself."

"You look after yourself, young lady, and remember you is never alone. You come up to the orphanage for your dinner any time you like."

Wilma engulfed Eleanor in a warm hug. She stood there, her hands by her side as the older woman squeezed her tight. Hugs weren't at all a thing in England not even for little children. She couldn't remember anyone ever hugging her before. It was different but in a nice way.

Wilma left quietly shutting the door behind her. Eleanor decided to go to bed, although it was relatively early. Today had been draining. She needed her strength to face Bertram Shaw tomorrow.

CHAPTER 33

The next few days passed without incident. Nothing was said of her comments to Bertram and the boy behaved himself. Well, as much as it was possible for a boy like him to do. Eleanor tried different ways to draw out the nicer side of the child but she couldn't find anything to work with. She met Mrs. Shaw once at the store. The woman had been hostile and would have snubbed her completely if she hadn't insisted on greeting Bertram first and then his mother. The poor boy didn't stand a chance with a mother like Mrs. Shaw.

She looked up at that moment to catch Gary watching her closely. He'd come down to the school with Laura's husband. Laura had introduced Eleanor to Paul Kelley, her husband. Gary had suggested they take advantage of his presence to head home early. School was nearly over and he would help to clear up.

Eleanor was about to protest when she saw Laura and Paul exchange a loving glance. So she insisted they go despite being wary of being alone with Gary. Not that they were alone given the number of children in school.

"Today was fun," Gary said as they tidied up the school house.

"It was but you honestly didn't need to stay. What about your own business?"

"I'm sure nobody but Murph missed me. Most cowboys wait until much later to start drinking," Gary explained, lifting some books and placing them back on the correct shelves.

"Who is Murph? Is that your cat?"

Gary laughed making Eleanor smile too. The beauty of her smile made him stop and stare at her. Before he could change his mind, he leaned in slowly allowing her time to withdraw before he gently brushed his lips against hers. She didn't move closer but at least she didn't push him away either. He took the book she was holding and put it down on the shelf beside him, then he drew her closer, not breaking eye contact. Her eyes widened as he leaned closer.

"I am going to kiss you again," he whispered softly, this time his lips grazing hers more firmly. She held herself rigid but he put his hands on her waist and drew her closer to him. She sighed, the sound thrilling him. He kissed her gently all over her face before moving back to her lips. They were just as soft as he expected them to be. This time, she moved closer to him, putting her arms around his neck as he deepened the kiss between them.

She was the one to break their connection, removing her arms and pushing him away.

"Sorry, someone may come in. I could lose my position." Her rapid breathing made her voice all husky.

He had to restrain the urge to take her back into his arms and show her just how much he wanted her.

"I am not sorry. I liked kissing you. I've wanted to do that from the first day we met."

"It was nice."

He moved toward her. "Nice?"

He could see she was flustered and for some reason he was thrilled. She wasn't immune to him despite playing the cold-blooded English miss.

"How nice?" he whispered, his lips almost at her ear.

"Lovely...but you have to stop now," she squeaked as he kissed her ear lobe. He could see her pulse beating quicker as he kissed her neck. She shivered and moaned, the sound nearly making him burst.

"Mr. Barrett, please stop," she murmured.

"I will if you really want me to, but I don't think you do. Do you?"

He nearly missed the small shake of her head. Smiling at her, he moved to her mouth and explored it once more. Then he cradled her to him.

"I want to spend all night kissing you, Eleanor."

She looked at him with such a wistful look on her face, his restraint nearly broke. He set her free, moving slowly away from her.

"We must think of your reputation. As we both know, gossip spreads like wildfire in this town."

She nodded but looked lost. He winked at her. "How about I walk you home? Mrs. Sullivan hasn't come back yet, has she?"

She stared at him.

"I will only walk you to the door. I assure you, my intentions are honorable. I won't do anything to make you the subject of gossip. I care too much for you to do that."

She smiled once more taking his breath away. "I think we are finished in here. Let's take that walk."

* * *

As they walked, he told her about his life story including moving to the USA from Britain as well as the recent problems with Dickinson.

"Oh, those poor girls. I can't imagine anyone being forced to work in a house of ill repute."

Eleanor's comment made Gary realize just how sheltered an upbringing she must have had. Surely, she didn't think girls grew up wanting to work as women of the night.

"According to the girls I have spoken to, most of them start that way. Then their families, hearing about how they have been living, don't want to know them. So they have no way out."

"Families can be so cruel," Eleanor said, her face a mask of sadness.

He wanted to hug her and tell her it would all be fine but he couldn't. They were in the middle of the street, but also, he didn't know if she would ever resolve things with her family.

* * *

They walked on in silence for a few minutes.

"You are the first one who hasn't asked me why I left England and came here," Eleanor said, a questioning look in her eyes. "The others weren't being nasty but I guess they were curious. You must be as well."

"I am but I figure you will tell me what I need to know when the time is right."

What did he mean by that? Had he seen the papers? No, if the news had reached Clover Springs, everyone would be talking about her.

"What? Why are you screwing up your face?" he asked smiling, but his eyes were wary.

"I just wondered what you meant when you said need to know."

"Well, if you ran away because you committed a murder, I guess you should tell me. Or if you followed a lover?"

Her cheeks warmed up at what he said. She'd never had a lover as he put it. Some of the young men she had grown up with flirted with her and asked her to dance but there had been no one serious.

"It wasn't for either of those reasons," she reassured him.

"Then, Eleanor, I don't care why you came to be in Clover Springs, I am just very glad you did."

He surprised her by lifting her hand and kissing it. Only then did she realize they had arrived at the boarding house.

"I would offer you coffee but I..." What could she say? She didn't trust herself to be alone with him. She wanted him to kiss her again? She couldn't admit to those things.

"There you are. I thought you had got lost. Oh, hello, Gary, didn't see you there. Would you like to come in?"

"No thank you, Mrs. Sullivan. I have to get back to work, to my real job."

Martha looked confused.

"Gary, I mean Mr. Barrett, helped me at the school as Laura went home early with her husband who happened to be in town. I wouldn't have managed without him."

"I hope you enjoyed it, Gary. Makes a change from the saloon."

"It did and it didn't. Some of my customers behave little better than children at times. Good day, Mrs. Sullivan and Miss Templeton. See you soon."

She stared at his retreating figure.

"Come inside, dear, and tell me all about it. You can't stand on the street looking like a lovesick young puppy. The gossips will love that."

Eleanor opened her mouth and shut it again as she realized Martha was teasing her. She went inside shutting the door, thankful her landlady was home.

* * *

Martha had baked a pie as a treat. "Thank you for keeping the place so well. You shouldn't have worked so hard."

"It was a pleasure and it gave me something to do. You have some beautiful furniture."

"I was married to a wonderful man who indulged me. We used to live on the ranch, but Davy and his wife, Mary, live there now with their children. I preferred to move into town."

"How is your daughter?"

"Elizabeth is much better now, thank you. I love my grandchildren but I am glad to be back in my own home. I felt bad about leaving you alone too."

"Everyone was very kind." Eleanor hastened to reassure her landlady.

"So I see. It didn't take long for you and Gary to start courting. He is a very nice man even if he does own a saloon."

"We aren't courting…" At Martha's raised eyebrow Eleanor couldn't continue.

"You like him a lot, don't you? He obviously likes you. I have never known him to spend too long away from the saloon."

"Yes, I like him but we aren't courting. I couldn't do that. I chose to be a teacher," Eleanor said firmly but whether it was to convince herself or Martha, she wasn't sure.

"Even a teacher is allowed to court, get married, and have a family," Martha said gently.

"Not this teacher. It is so lovely having you back."

"You have a very kind heart, Eleanor. One that deserves to be loved and nurtured. Don't make the mistake of putting your career above everything else. Just because one man broke your heart doesn't mean the next one will."

Martha kissed her on the cheek before taking her shawl off the hook. "I won't be long. I want to run over to check on my other grandchildren. I have missed Katie and my Ella and Danny. Don't worry about clearing up. I will do that when I come back. I have to go now or they will be in bed."

"I will clear up. Thank you very much for the pie and your kindness."

Martha closed the door behind her leaving Eleanor alone with her thoughts. What would Martha think if she knew the man who broke her heart wasn't a suitor but her father?

She cleared the table, washed the dishes and put them away. Martha hadn't returned so she went up to her room. She was going to write another letter to Gracie. Maybe Lady Devon wouldn't see it. She wished she had a way to send letters in secret, but then she had never had to be devious before. How she wished Gracie was here in Clover Springs. She could talk to her about Mr. Barrett. Gary. She'd enjoyed the kiss more than she should of. In England, she had been heavily chaperoned, as were all the young ladies she knew. They weren't allowed be alone with any man unless he was a father or brother or in some cases if the chaperone was feeling lenient, a fiancé. She didn't have much experience with the opposite sex never mind kissing.

Well brought up ladies were supposed to endure the physical side of the relationship. She wasn't exactly sure what that entailed but if it was as nice as kissing, she couldn't understand her grandmother's dire warnings.

What she wouldn't give to have someone to talk to. She wanted to kiss Gary again. But she couldn't. He might think they had a future together and that was out of the question.

CHAPTER 34

The next week flew by. The gossip in town was all about Doc Erin and her friends getting stuck in New York. The reason they hadn't heard from them was not because they were having so much fun but because all the telegraph wires had blown down. Mrs. Grey had finally received a message to say they would all be home soon.

Gary tried to see as much of Eleanor as he could. He got up early so he could walk her to the school house which was silly really given the short distance between the boarding house and school. He always had some excuse about going to see Father Molloy or collecting things from the store. He thought Eleanor knew what he was doing but they didn't discuss it. They didn't get a chance to be alone again so he couldn't kiss her as much as he wanted to.

She seemed to be relaxing a little in his company, although she still refused to tell him anything about her family. She spoke about her father's time in India, and told him funny stories about the Prince of Wales whose lifestyle was giving his mother, Queen Victoria, more grey hairs. If he ever probed about her family, she shut down fast. He had learned not to ask. Despite not knowing much of her personal history, he knew he loved and wanted to marry her.

* * *

GARY CHECKED his reflection over and over. Did he look right? He'd never asked anyone to marry him before so wanted it to be perfect. He hadn't seen her in a few days but had heard of the roasting she gave young Bertram. He'd deserved it too. That boy could do with a sound clip around the ears. He'd wanted to call to the boarding house and reassure Eleanor she was doing a good job but that would mean admitting there was gossip about her in town. If they were married, he could protect her. He wouldn't expect her to stop working, but he could be there when she came home in the evening.

Taking his hat and the book he had picked out for Eleanor, he left his lodgings over the saloon and walked to the boarding house. Flowers would have been better but there were none this time of year. He thought she might enjoy reading something American. He wasn't just in love with her physical appearance, it was her mind and her character that intrigued him. The conversations they had enjoyed had left him wanting more. As for the strong physical attraction, he was only human and marriage couldn't come quick enough.

Taking a big breath, he knocked on the door. Mrs. Sullivan had come back late yesterday, so he wasn't surprised to see her open it. "Come in, please, Gary. I take it you are here to see Eleanor?"

"Yes, please, ma'am." Gary's mouth was dry.

"Why don't you go into the sitting room and I will call her. Would you like something to drink?" Martha asked.

"I'll just help myself to some water, if that's all right?" Gary asked suddenly thirsty.

"You go ahead, love. I must say you look very fetching all dressed up."

Gary blushed at her good-natured teasing but it quickly disappeared when Eleanor came into the room. She looked terrified.

"Miss Templeton, Eleanor, I…brought you this." He handed her the book.

"*Little Women*. I have heard of this. What a lovely gift, thank you," Eleanor said shyly, not looking at him.

Her eyes were a little less wary, but she was still holding herself rigid. He'd thought they had made some progress. They had kissed after all, and she seemed to enjoy the experience as much as he did.

He couldn't wait any longer. He went down on one knee and immediately knew by the horrified look on her face, her answer was going to be no.

"Eleanor, will you please be my wife?"

"Gary, get up, please. Before Mrs. Sullivan walks in. Please. I'm sorry but you have mistaken my affection. I…can't marry you."

"Can't or won't?"

"I won't ever marry anyone. I'm sorry but that is my final word."

"Can you tell me why?" Gary asked, not quite believing what she was saying.

"It's none of your business."

"I am making it my business. I love you, Eleanor Templeton, and I believe you love me. So why won't you marry me? Is it because of the saloon? I can sell it."

"No, it's not that."

"So what is it?"

"You want to have children."

"Yes, so? You love children, I've seen you with them at school. You are a natural mother. You can't deny it."

"Yes, I love them but…" She turned her back to him.

"Tell me. But what?" Gary pushed her for an answer.

"But nothing. I have said no, what more do you want?"

She didn't wait for an answer but left him standing there as she ran up the stairs. He was still staring after her when Mrs. Sullivan came in.

"I take it she said no," Martha said.

"How did you know I planned on asking her?"

"The love you two share is written all over your faces. She told me how you helped her when I was away. She loves you, Gary, but she is terrified."

"Of me? I would never hurt her."

"I know that, but somebody did and until she gets over it, she will never trust anyone again."

"So I am wasting my time?" Gary asked, hoping she would say no.

"I didn't say that, lad. True love is worth waiting for. Just have a little patience."

* * *

ELEANOR CRIED into her pillow hoping it would muffle the sound. She heard Martha calling to her and knocking on the door, but she had pretended she was asleep. She couldn't face the kind woman. Closing her eyes, she could see his face, the look of pain and confusion in his eyes. She loved him but she couldn't ever be his wife. She couldn't risk inflicting a miserable future on both of them and any children they may be blessed with. Since Wilma had given her talk about slavery at the school, Eleanor had spoken in private with her and Jane. The young girl had told Eleanor what it was like to live as a black woman in Denver. It had taken some time before Jane opened up about the real reason she was here.

Eleanor couldn't believe such a violent and unprovoked crime would not be investigated but it wasn't. The Denver police department weren't interested. It made Eleanor's blood boil. Unusual for her, especially as she had always stayed out of politics in England. Well, apart from to voice her support of Home Rule in Ireland but that had only been to her father and his friends.

Wilma encouraged Eleanor to spend time with Jane. Jane was fascinated by Eleanor's clothes so she spent some time in her room trying various dresses on. One in particular—a white ball gown Eleanor hadn't been able to leave behind—was beautiful on Jane. The girl was so thin she didn't really need a corset, but Eleanor used it anyway. She wouldn't let Jane see the result until she had her fully dressed. When the young girl saw her reflection, it made her cry. Eleanor had seen John, Rosa's older brother, on the street and sent him to get Wilma. Wilma returned with Ellen in tow, and they were as mesmerized with Jane's appearance as she was.

"You look so beautiful. Your Rev. Douglass would burst a gut if he saws you in that."

"Why doesn't he? Wilma, you could invite him for the Easter ball and if Eleanor didn't mind Jane could borrow the dress. We could all dress up for the night."

Eleanor watched Jane's face. The girl was battling her demons but hope seemed to be winning.

"I don't want to lend Jane the dress," Eleanor said, making everyone stare at her.

Jane fingered the dress wistfully before she said, "I understand, Eleanor, it's far too nice for someone like me anyways."

"I want to give you the dress, Jane. It was made for you."

Jane's eyes widened as Ellen and Wilma clapped.

"I can't take a dress like this."

"Yes, you can and you will. It is fabulous and your young man will be mesmerized."

"Are you sure?"

"Very sure, Jane. You look incredible."

Jane went back to staring at her reflection. Wilma came over to hug Eleanor, and this time, she was able to hug the older woman back.

"You is gettin' there, girl. Trusting people takes courage and you have that in bucketfuls."

"Thank you, Wilma. I have my own story to tell you. Would you all stay to tea. I would like Martha to be there too."

"We'll stay. I will help Jane out of this dress, and you go find Martha. We will be done in just a few minutes."

Martha was more than willing to put on some coffee and set out cookies. She even made some tea for Eleanor who hadn't yet got to grips with the American fascination for coffee.

"I want you all to know I am very thankful for your friendship. You have all been so kind to me since I arrived in Clover Springs a few weeks ago. It seems like I have lived here a long time." Eleanor stopped speaking as she looked down at her hands. Could she do this? There was no putting the cat back in the bag once she told her story.

Wilma coughed. "You can do this, girl, go on."

"I am not English, although my accent suggests I am. I was born here in the USA somewhere in the deep South. My mother was a slave."

CHAPTER 35

The silence screamed in the room as they all stared at her. Ellen opened her mouth to speak but closed it again. Wilma smiled at her encouraging her to take the next step. Martha stared at her, shocked into silence while Jane gripped Eleanor's hand tightly. She squeezed Jane's hand as she began to speak.

"Yes, my skin color suggests I am white but it seems this can happen when your mother is only part black as was her mother before her. I am not sure how many generations you have to go back before you find my ancestors look just like Wilma and Jane." Eleanor smiled at the two ladies before taking a drink of her tea.

"I never knew my background. My father was very friendly with the Prince of Wales, and as a result, we moved in the highest of high society back in England. My father's wife was a lady in her own right, her father being an earl. I was treated much the same as other children in our circle. In England, this means Nanny brings you up but you see your parents for an hour at dinner."

"I read things like that in books, but I can't see how any mother could leave her child to be raised by others when she is living with them. Don't seem natural to me," Martha said shaking her head. Ellen squeezed her hand and told her to be quiet making Eleanor smile.

"As I grew older, I started to notice little things. My half-sisters were adored by our grandmother, my father's mother, but she seemed to take pleasure in finding fault with me. I didn't care much as my father, possibly seeing what was happening, insisted I spend more time with him. He sent me to Cheltenham Ladies College, he said it would brighten my future and give me options. I think it was his way of preparing me for what could happen."

"Where is he now?"

"Martha Sullivan, you been spending too much time with Mary," Wilma spluttered. "Will you stop asking questions and let the girl talk. Go on, Eleanor."

"My father asked the Prince of Wales to request I be presented at court. My grandmother nearly had a fit but it was a royal command so she couldn't do anything about it. I thought she had given her consent as I wore her diamonds. I only found out later my father had borrowed them without her knowledge. Anyway, it was rather a disaster. Most of the young men in our set prefer blonde, blue-eyed girls with the palest of skin." Eleanor's voice quivered as she remembered the humiliation of having to spend the night dancing with her father or one of the prince's friends.

"My father died suddenly a few months ago. We didn't know he was ill, although looking back, the signs were there. When he died, my grandmother summoned me to her house. She gave me two weeks to leave London, booking me a cabin on a ship sailing to Boston. She wrote me a letter of introduction to Mrs. Gantley whose husband had known my father years ago."

"Why would she do something so horrible?" Martha asked in tears.

"She told me the story of my life as she knew it. According to her, my mother was the daughter of one of the house slaves. You know after the war, many of the people who had been slaves stayed working at the same plantations. Seems this is what my mama did. She got pregnant and blamed my father, or the man I consider my father. My father wanted to do the honorable thing and marry her. Seems he had fallen in love. Can you imagine the scandal? Anyway, I don't know what happened to her or where I grew up for the first four years of my life, but he took me with him when we left America. First, he traveled across Europe and we spent many wonderful years together. I had people to look after me but he always made time for me. Then we went back to England, he married my stepmother and everything changed. So there you have it. That is the reason why I left Britain."

"And why you won't marry Gary," Wilma stated.

Shocked, Eleanor didn't know what to say. How did Wilma know about that?

"Gary hasn't said nothin' but I seen his sad face. His smile done disappeared for a reason. And you have been miserable too. So I put two and two together and made a guess. You just confirmed it."

"You tricked me"

"Yes, Eleanor I did. Now tell us why you won't marry a good man who is crazy about you and you in love with him."

"Wilma, you know I can't."

"I know nothin' of the sort."

"What if we have children?"

"That would be a blessing wouldn't it, or are you sick of them at school already?"

Everyone laughed, even Jane.

"I think Miss Eleanor be scared the baby might be black." Jane's statement shocked the women. Not because of what she said but because she was talking. She usually kept quiet, especially in company. "What you all looking at, I got a voice. I just don't use it much." She smiled.

"Is that true, Eleanor?"

"Yes. What if we had a baby and it was black. That can happen, can't it Wilma?"

"I guess so, child. I can't remember ever seeing or hearing of a white couple having a black baby, but I did see black children being born to pale mothers who were the masters."

"You mean the master made the slave pregnant."

"Yes, Miss Ellen. Don't you be listening to me?" Wilma said but her tone was teasing. "I think there is a risk, but, Eleanor, wouldn't you love the baby just the same?"

Eleanor's eyes watered. "Of course I would, Wilma, but what would people around here think? Nobody is going to believe the baby would be my husband's. It would make our lives miserable."

"No, child, the gossips would do that. So long as you tell Gary the truth, there is nothing stopping you from having a happy future. I ain't known Gary long but I know him well enough to know color don't bother him none. He adores Rosa and she would spend all day in that saloon if I didn't chase her out of there."

"He rescued her at school one day and he was so kind. I think I knew then I loved him," Eleanor smiled wistfully.

"Child, take a lesson from an old woman like me. There ain't much happiness in the world. It sure isn't going to walk up to your front door demanding you take a hold of it. You got to grab it as soon as you can and never let go. You got to do that with Gary. Go see him, tell him you made a mistake and why."

"I couldn't do that. I can't go chasing a man?"

"Why? Because of what your grandmama might say? I thought you was an educated woman. If your grandmama thinks it is all right to throw your family out on the street then her opinion ain't worth nothin'."

"Wilma's right. You have to explain to Gary. At least give him the real reason you turned him down. He is so miserable right now," Martha added. "Murph complained he had to drink at home as Gary was turning the whiskey sour."

The others laughed while Eleanor stared silently at Wilma. The older woman touched her on the arm.

"What you thinking about?" Wilma asked her softly.

"I wonder is it possible to find out what happened to my mama? What if she isn't dead like they said. Maybe I have a family out there somewhere."

Wilma held her hand tight. "I just happen to know

some people who can help, but Jane knows them much better. Why don't the rest of us carry on with our business, and Jane can take you upstairs and tell you about her grandma and the work she did to reunite ex-slaves. You two is about the same age. Ellen has to go home to Jake, I want my bed, and I guess Martha has work she could be doing."

Eleanor would have smiled at the look on Martha's face if it was any other time. The older woman clearly wanted to hear Jane's story, too, but a look from Wilma convinced her she should leave Jane and her alone. Jane followed her upstairs and together they took off the ball gown. Jane told Eleanor stories about her gran and the slaves she had reunited. Obviously, not all the stories had happy endings but some of them did. One thing Jane warned Eleanor about was the fact her family, if she did find them, may not be too accepting of her.

"Some of our people can't abide white people, no matter what age they are or who their parents was," Jane sighed. "Racism grows on both sides of the fence and you is caught right bang in the middle."

CHAPTER 36

Wilma took her time walking to the school, enjoying the winter sunlight. She hadn't slept well, her mind turning over Eleanor's story. In her dreams, Eleanor had become Solace even though it was impossible. Eleanor was too young for a start. She wondered about Eleanor's father's motives for taking the child back to Britain. Perhaps he believed her fair skin would protect her. Looking at her, you wouldn't imagine her heritage. When she stood next to Ellen, there were some similarities and some differences. They shared the same jet-black hair but where Ellen had pale, sallow skin, Eleanor's had more of a honey color, as if she had spent time sunbathing. Wilma didn't know much about the aristocracy in Britain, but she knew the ladies of the Southern plantations had abhorred sunbathing. The paler one's skin the better. Eleanor's eyes were the color of dark wood but again unless you were looking for signs of race, you wouldn't comment on them.

She hoped the girl would take their advice and put her past behind her. Gary Barrett was a pleasant, intelligent young man with a kind heart. He'd shown what he was made of by refusing to work for Dickinson. He'd been run out of town but he'd come back as soon as he could, and his testimony helped convict Dickinson. She liked Gary and thought he would be a good match for Eleanor.

Wilma smiled as she saw the children climbing the steps as they returned to school following lunch. Walking quicker, she tried to catch up with the last of them. She didn't want to be late. She enjoyed working at the school and she learned something new every day. It reminded her of the lessons her mama had given her back when she was a child. It always happened late at night because the master had strictly forbidden his slaves to learn to read. Mama had insisted on teaching her saying it was the only true route to freedom and was worth any cost. Had it been, really? The master had discovered what Mama was doing. Instead of killing her, he had caused her more pain by selling her daughter and grandchild. If it weren't for Mama teaching slaves to read, Wilma might never have been on the auction block with

Solace. She would not have caused Zack to be enslaved. They wouldn't have been sold to the new master and she might not have met the captain.

"Miss Wilma, you came to school again. I love when you are here."

"Thank you, petal, I love being with you too, Rosa."

Wilma concentrated on the child, she was the future. The past needed to stay where it belonged.

* * *

"AFTERNOON, children, thank you for all coming back so promptly after lunch. Miss Wilma is here to help me again today."

"Thank you, Miss Eleanor, I am really looking forward to being with you all," Wilma said as she walked through the classroom. She picked up John's slate. "I love math." The children giggled as she made a funny face. It was common knowledge Wilma preferred just about anything to math.

Just then Gary arrived in the door. "Sorry for interrupting you all. Wilma, there is a very distinguished gentleman sitting in the orphanage waiting for you."

"Me? Who is it?" Wilma asked as she handed the slate back to young John.

"He says his name is Jackman. Says you would know who he was."

"Typical man. How's I meant to know who he is when I is never heard of no Mr. Jackman? Gary, what he look like?"

"Wilma, don't take your temper out on me. I was told to pass on a message and that's all I am doing."

"Sorry, Gary. I didn't mean to take your head off only I don't like strangers askin' for me. It usually means trouble."

"I don't know this man but he don't look like trouble," Gary responded carefully. "Why don't you go and see?"

"I will, after school ends. I can't leave Eleanor here on her own."

"I can help Miss Templeton," Gary responded as Eleanor said, "I am fine, Wilma. Please go and see your visitor."

"Think you should go, Miss Wilma. Gary and Miss Eleanor might want some time on their own," Rosa piped up. "They are good friends most of the time, although they fight a bit."

The class laughed as both Gary and Eleanor turned red. Wilma smiled and patted Rosa on the head.

"I guess I got to go then. Rosa, I will see you later."

CHAPTER 37

Wilma walked slowly toward the orphanage. Who could the man be? Someone who had followed her from Boston? No, they wouldn't come into the orphanage and ask for her by name. The type she'd known would skulk around.

She met Mrs. Grey coming out of the store.

"Wilma, what's wrong? Where's your usual smile?"

"There be someone waitin' for me in the kitchen. A man."

"So? Why are you looking scared? What's he said?"

"Nothin' as far as I know. Gary Barrett said he seemed a nice man. But what does he want with me?"

"Will I come with you?"

"Would you? I know I is being silly but..."

"I'm coming. I need a coffee and anyway the

curiosity will kill me." Mrs. Grey smiled as she took Wilma's arm and the two of them made their way to the orphanage in silence.

Wilma pushed the door open slowly as if expecting to get bit. Sitting at the table was Zack. He looked so different, he was wearing a suit. Like a real gentleman. Wilma looked to Mrs. Grey but she was staring at Zack too, her mouth open.

"Miss Wilma, there you are. I am real sorry to intrude on you this way. I meant to send a telegram but I thought it better to just turn up."

"You are very welcome to my home, Zack. You know my friend Mrs. Grey and I guess you and Samuel have got acquainted." Wilma was dying to ask just how well they had got on and, more importantly, what they talked about but she couldn't do that.

"Zack, it was lovely speaking to you. I have to get outside and do my chores now or Wilma will have words with me. I will walk you to the boarding house later," Samuel said before limping toward the door heading for the garden. "You coming, Mrs. Grey?"

"No, she's staying for coffee," Wilma answered on behalf of Mrs. Grey. She didn't want to be alone with Zack. She wasn't afraid of him, instinctively she knew he wouldn't hurt her, not on purpose. But she had ruined the man's life.

He must hold it against her.

"Wilma, Zack may wish to speak to you in private. I will go home. See you later."

"NO!"

"Mrs. Grey, please sit down. It might be good for Wilma to have a friend with her. I have some news, not all of it is good." Zack's concern caused them all to stare at him.

Wilma slumped into the chair. Samuel looked strained as if unsure whether he should stay or go. Mrs. Grey put down her bag and started making some coffee.

"Mr. Samuel, it might be best if you left us alone. I am not sure how much Wilma wishes her friends to know but I will leave that to her to decide."

"Yes, of course. I am out back if you need me. Lock the door and then the children will have to use the other entrance."

"Thank you."

Wilma still couldn't say anything. She listened to them talking but it was hard to hear what they were saying over the roar of her heart beating. She tried taking some deep breathes. He had news—some good and some bad. She wanted the bad news first.

"Tell me."

"I think we should wait until Mrs. Grey sits down." Zack took Wilma's hand in his. "You must be brave. I know you are a strong woman."

"I ain't. Not anymore."

"Yes, you are. As strong as you were all those years ago in that cage. I can see it in you." He spoke so softly only she could hear him. She looked up amazed to see admiration in his eyes. "You are the woman I have dreamed of. I thought I would never find you."

Dreamed of? Find? What on earth was he talking about? She had only met him that one time when she'd ruined him. She could feel the heat bearing down on them as they sat in the cage for two or was it three days. Zack had sat with her and Solace, his presence helping to protect them from the attention of some young males. They had shared their stories, and it had helped pass the time. Zack had told her of his plans to take over his parent's business, although he had admitted he may go up North when the war was over.

"Drink this, Wilma. It will help a little." Mrs. Grey handed Wilma a full cup. She then gave Zack one and took a seat, her cup in front of her.

"Tell me, please. The bad news? Is Solace dead?"

"Yes, she is. I'm sorry. She died a year ago."

"Only last year. Why didn't I start looking for her sooner? I could have been there. I could have helped her. Why?" Wilma kept asking, tears running down her face.

"I don't think you would have found her, Wilma,

and in many ways, it is better you didn't. She was living as a white woman."

"A white woman? But…Why?"

"I don't have all the answers to that. Her friend Andrew was killed when they tried to escape. Someone found Solace and offered her shelter. She joined their family and in time married one of their relations. I gather she never told them she was a runaway slave. They assumed she be white. She told them she'd been separated by her family by the war."

"As so many were," Mrs. Grey added.

"Was she happy? Please tell me my little girl was happy?" Wilma begged him.

He didn't say anything for a minute and then he looked at her.

"She wasn't, was she?"

"She was, I believe for some time. But then she had a family. Twin girls."

"I am a grandma. A real one."

She looked at Mrs. Grey but her friend's eyes were glued to Zack's, her face white as snow.

"What? Why are you looking at him like that?" Wilma asked Mrs. Grey. Her answer was to take Wilma's hand and squeeze it.

"Tell me," Wilma demanded.

"I guess there was something wrong with the babies," Mrs. Grey said in a very shaky voice.

"Wrong? They died? Oh, my poor baby."

Zack cleared his throat. "There was in the eyes of Solace's husband. One baby was born white but the other—"

"Was born black," Mrs. Grey interrupted.

"Yes. Solace's husband accused her of having an affair with a local black man. The rest of the story is not pleasant."

"Tell me," Wilma ordered, holding onto Mrs. Grey's hand for dear life.

"Solace tried to tell her husband the truth, but he wouldn't listen. Instead, he and a group of his friends dragged the man he suspected of being unfaithful with his wife away from his home and family and killed him. Then he turned his anger on the baby. He would have killed her, too, if Solace hadn't stopped him. Solace's mother-in-law, suspecting Solace was telling the truth, grabbed the child and ran. Solace was left alone with her husband. He beat her. Badly. She never regained the use of her legs after the attack. He threw her out along with both children."

When he stopped talking the only sound in the kitchen was Mrs. Grey sobbing quietly. Wilma couldn't cry. She couldn't believe what she was hearing.

"How do you know all this?"

"I lived quite near Solace. I didn't realize it until the

community started talking. Of course, people preferred to think she had an affair rather than duped them. I went to speak to her. I brought her back to where I lived and we looked after her. She didn't speak much. Would never talk about the past."

"So how do you know this woman was my daughter?" Wilma demanded. 'There is a chance you are mistaken and Solace is alive out there somewhere."

"I am sorry, but there isn't. She told my wife the whole story just before she died. She wanted her to take the children."

"Did she?"

His face turned hard, a look of disgust in his eyes.

"My wife didn't want a white child. She said she would take one of them."

"After everything my poor Solace had been through?"

"Yes, my wife or should I say ex-wife still carries a lot of anger. All of it is directed at white people even innocent young children. She doesn't care the baby is deemed black due to her parentage."

"So where are the children?" Mrs. Grey asked as Wilma was trying to make sense of the loss of her child.

"They live at the orphanage with Reverend Douglass."

Wilma turned on him. "You mean I had family

there all the time and you didn't tell me. Was this your revenge. In return for my ruining your life?"

"Wilma, I have no idea what you are talking about. You never ruined my life. As for the children, I didn't know the story. When you told of your search, I remembered the girl. She said her name was Sarah. I knew her to be about the right age. I went to see my ex-wife to find out more. It was only then I found out the truth. I went back to the orphanage to check the children haven't been adopted."

"Were they?"

"That is the good news and reason for my visit. They are still in the orphanage. I assume you want to collect them and bring them home."

Wilma couldn't speak. She could barely think. She stared at him.

"I would have brought them but I thought it was too much for you to take in. And the children…they have been through so much already. I didn't want them disappointed again."

"How would they be?" Wilma demanded. Could he really believe she wouldn't want her baby's children? They were her flesh and blood. Her family.

"Well, if you said no or if you decided to only have one."

Wilma stood up so fast the chair fell backwards. "Are you saying you thought I might turn them away?

Or not take one because she looks white? Is that what you is saying?"

"Wilma, calm down. Your heart…" Mrs. Grey interjected.

"My heart be fine. I want my grandchildren. Both of them! Do you hear me? I want them with me. They is my family," Wilma screamed.

CHAPTER 38

Eleanor looked at Gary under her eyelashes. He was helping John figure out his math. He was so patient taking his time to explain the problem slowly. He glanced up catching her staring at him, the look he gave her making her insides melt. Their gazes caught for a couple of seconds before he turned his attention back to the child.

It seemed to take forever before it was time to release the children from school. She almost gave into temptation to let them go early but that would only cause talk. She paced up and down the aisles picking up and cleaning the same slates.

"Miss Eleanor, that's the third time you cleaned my slate. You is like a buzzy bee today."

The other children laughed at Sarah's comments

but Eleanor barely registered it. She kept glancing at the clock and as soon as it was time, rang the bell. The noise of the children pushing back their seats and filing out of the room seemed to be happening in the distance as her gaze was centered on Gary. Soon they would be alone together for the first time since he proposed.

She fidgeted with her hands, wiping them on her skirt before fidgeting all over again. Part of her wanted to make an excuse and follow the children, the other part knew she should stay. Wilma and the other ladies had been right. She did love him and she owed him a chance to make his choice. He was a good, kind, decent man and they didn't grow on trees.

"Eleanor, stop fidgeting, you are making me nervous. I won't propose again if that's what you are worried about." Although he smiled, his eyes reminded her of a dog back home in England. He had been mistreated by his owner but still followed him everywhere in the hope it would turn out good. It never did.

"Gary, sit down, please. I need to speak to you."

Gary took a seat at one of the children's desks but he looked so silly, a grown man trying to fit into the small place, she giggled. Then she stopped. How could she laugh at a time like this?

"Maybe we should stand?" he suggested.

He came closer to her, she took a step back and another but he kept coming. Soon, her back was against the wall and there was nowhere for her to go.

"Eleanor, please. You look terrified. Whatever you have to say, can it wait one minute?"

She gazed at his face, her eyes focusing on his lips. Surprising herself, she reached up and touched her lips to his. He pulled her into his arms, his mouth taking hers in a kiss. A kiss like no other.

Breathing hard, she placed her hands on his chest to push him away. "I must talk to you. There are things you should know."

He put both his hands under her face, holding her chin in his palms, forcing her to look up at him.

"I love you. I think you love me. That's all I need to know."

He kissed her again but this time it was a kiss of such gentleness it was as if a butterfly had flown across her lips.

"You don't have to tell me anything, but I will do my best to listen if you really want to talk. I'd prefer to kiss," he whispered as he continued to drop feather kisses on her lips.

She giggled as he kissed her all over her face.

"I like kissing you, too, but I want you to know why I turned you down. Stop doing that, you're distracting me," she whispered as he kissed the base of her ear while his hands massaged the back of her head. Her hair was falling down.

"Gary!"

Her tone got his attention and he stepped back from her. "You shouldn't be so tempting. Your hair is so silky I want to see it flowing down your back covering your…"

"Gary Barrett, will you stop." Mortified, she turned away, although his words had a funny effect on her stomach. She couldn't think straight.

"My children may turn out black," she blurted, watching his face closely. His eyes widened in surprise. "That's why I can't marry you."

He turned her gently back to look at him, his hands remaining on her shoulders.

"What are your saying?"

"I can't marry you. What if I had a child who looked like Rosa? The town would think I had betrayed you, or at least they would if there were any black men in town."

"Wait a minute. What do you mean your children could turn out black? I don't understand," Gary said quietly before kissing her on the forehead. "Eleanor, darling, I am not rejecting you. I just need you to explain."

She took a risk to look him in the eyes. Did he

mean it? Or was she just hearing what she longed to hear. Someone who loved her despite everything. The love in his eyes encouraged her to speak.

"My mother was a slave. I inherited my father's coloring. He was white. The son of a rich woman who threw me out before his body got cold. It was only then I found out what my heritage was. She spelled it out quite plainly what could happen to me in the future, to my children. Most of all, she made it clear, she wasn't taking the risk of having any of her relations any other color than white."

Shocked, he didn't know what to say. How could anyone be so cruel? "Why didn't your father tell you? You were old enough by the time he died."

"Yes, I was almost twenty. I don't know why he didn't tell me, and I have asked myself that over and over. If I had known, I could have protected myself from my grandmother and the rest of my family. Him dying was bad enough. I lost the father I adored, but I also lost all meaning in my life. I don't care about the money or the privilege but I lost my identity. Who am I? Who is my mother? Is she really dead like I was told? Or did she run away? Did he send her away knowing what I now know about his family? All these questions and the one person who can answer them is dead."

He took his arms from the top of her shoulders.

For a split second, she thought he was going to leave her. Instead, he pulled her so close she could barely breathe. He held her like that, stroking her back for a little while, kissing the top of her head a couple of times.

"Eleanor, I can't imagine the pain of what you have been through, but your story makes no difference to how I feel about you. I love you and God forbid if I got hold of your grandmother I might just shake her."

"You really don't mind?"

"Mind? Darling, your background makes you unique. You are special. I don't know why your father left your mother, she may have died. Or he may have realized she didn't belong in his world. But either way, he loved you enough to not want to give you up. I love you and I will never give you up."

"But…"

"There are no buts. I would marry you right now if I could," he insisted.

She stood in silence, his love for her flowing from his eyes to hers.

"I want to find out what happened to my family… Mama's family."

"Of course you do. She may still be alive. You could have siblings. Or aunts and uncles. There must be someone who knows." He looked down at her. "I will help you find your family. But I have a condition."

"What?" She couldn't stop the fear crawling up her spine into her voice.

"I want us to be married first. I don't want anyone objecting to us getting married."

"Why would anyone care who I married?" she asked wonderingly.

"You are so innocent and that is part of why I love you. There is a lot of bad feeling in the world and some of that is directed against people because of their color."

"But you are white," she was confused.

"Exactly, and you could have a big black uncle with muscles on his muscles who doesn't like white men, particularly those with designs on his niece."

Eleanor giggled. "You are funny."

"I am actually serious. There is racism on both sides. After reading *Uncle Tom's Cabin,* I can understand why."

Eleanor thought of Jane and her horrific experience. Yes, she guessed she could understand too. She held onto Gary tighter. She wasn't about to let another family member destroy her future. But maybe he was saying that about her mama's family to give him an excuse to leave her. Maybe he...

"Did your father have any siblings? Or best friends? Someone who spent time in the US with him?"

"Don't you think I haven't thought of all those

options. Nobody will speak to me. I don't even know where my father lived when he was here," she snapped back, her terror of him leaving her taking over.

* * *

HE HEARD the terror in her voice as he felt her body shaking. His anger threatened to spill over. What sort of old witch could treat her own grandchild so badly her confidence was so low? How could he make her believe he loved her and didn't care where she came from so long as she lived the rest of her life at his side. He kissed her gently on the forehead. Then he pushed her away and knelt on one knee in front of her.

"What are you doing?" she squeaked.

"Eleanor, please look at me. I know you have been treated abdominally by your family and everyone you held dear. But I love you. I want to marry you. I want to have children with you. I don't care what color they are. They can be green-haired with red freckles for all I care. I will love them almost as much as I love you."

She looked into his eyes. He wanted to chase away the fear and pain lurking in their depths. "I swear I will never hurt you. Not knowingly or intentionally."

"But what about the gossip if we do have children?" she whispered, her voice quivering with emotion.

"So what? Let people talk. They do it anyway. We don't have to listen to it. We don't have to stay in Clover Springs. We can move anywhere you want."

"I like it here."

"So do I, but I will live with you wherever you want. So, Miss Eleanor Templeton, is that a yes?"

She looked up at him, her eyes full of hope and trust. He sucked in his breath, hoping he would never ever let her down. He would do everything in his power to make her believe in herself—in both of them.

"I'm waiting rather impatiently. I want to get back to kissing." He waggled his eyebrows at her trying to make her smile.

She reached up and pulled him down to kiss her. This time, he let her lead the kiss following her pace, although it took all his self-control not to plunder her mouth and make her his.

They broke apart, both breathing hard, clinging to each other as if drowning in the sea.

"I take it that is a yes?"

"Yes, Mr. Barrett. It's a yes."

He picked her up and spun her around so fast she got dizzy.

"Who will we tell first?"

"Wilma. She knows my story and she said she would help me if I wanted to look for my family."

"Only once we are married. Remember your uncle?" He held out his arm trying to flex his muscles.

"I think you might want to get to exercising, darling, if you have to fight for me," she teased.

"Anything for you, m'lady."

CHAPTER 39

THE ORPHANAGE

Hearing Wilma shout, Ellen rushed down the stairs and into the kitchen.

"Wilma, what's wrong? Why are you shouting? Who are you? What did you say to make her like this? Didn't you know she'd been unwell?" Ellen fired questions at Zack as she cuddled Wilma who was sobbing as if her heart was broken.

"Ellen, calm down," Mrs. Grey suggested. "Wilma got some bad news and some wonderful news. Zack is Wilma's friend. They first met back in eighteen sixty-two."

"You did? I can't remember her talking about you," Ellen said trying not to be rude but she was angry at the state Wilma was in. Scared too if she was honest. She didn't want Wilma collapsing again.

"Tilly, can you go for Father Molloy, please. Ask

him to come immediately." Mrs. Grey took charge. "Ellen, can you include everyone for dinner? I must go to the boarding house and check there is a room ready for Zack to stay. He is staying here for one night and then the three of us will be returning to Denver in the morning."

"You are going away again?" Ellen said, completely astounded by what was happening in her kitchen. Wilma never left Clover Springs. She'd only come back from her trip to Denver and she was off again. "I don't think Wilma is well enough, Mrs. Grey."

"Ellen, you are the school teacher. I am the nurse. Now please trust me to know what is best for Wilma. Zack, would you like to come with me? I can show you the boarding house, and it will give Wilma some time to speak to Father Molloy."

The strange man stood up, not taking his eyes off Wilma.

"Can I please return later?" he asked.

Ellen was about to say no, but Wilma nodded her head.

"Thank you. I am very sorry to upset you so much." His eyes were glistening, his face full of concern causing Ellen to wonder about his motives. Why would he upset Wilma when he obviously cared for her?

Ellen waited for Wilma to respond but she said nothing.

"I think you should go," Ellen said coldly. "I don't understand what happened here but Wilma has been a friend of mine for a long time. I won't have her upset like this."

"Ellen, your loyalty does you credit but have a little patience. None of this is Zack's fault. In fact, Wilma owes him a great deal," Mrs. Grey said sharply.

Ellen's mouth fell open as she watched Mrs. Grey escort the stranger off the premises. Mrs. Grey was Wilma's closest friend, yet she had defended the man who upset her. Ellen wished Doc Erin was back from New York but bad weather had kept them there.

She continued to hold Wilma as the older woman cried. Ellen was crying, too, although she didn't understand what was wrong. But it was impossible not to be emotional at the sound of Wilma's heart breaking. The door opened admitting a shocked looking Father Molloy. He motioned to Ellen to bring Wilma to the sitting room where they could speak in private. She did and then she left them alone. Reluctantly, she closed the door giving them privacy. She knew Father Molloy would help Wilma.

CHAPTER 40

Samuel came back in as Ellen closed the door of the sitting room. They walked through to the kitchen.

"Is Zack gone?" Samuel asked.

"What do you know about that man?"

Samuel's look told Ellen her tone was too sharp.

"Sorry, Samuel, but I came down from my nap to witness Wilma crying like her heart was broken and Mrs. Grey defending the stranger who made Wilma cry."

"He seemed like a nice man. He came looking for Wilma but she was down at the school. Gary happened to be here so he went to get her while I entertained Zack. He said he knew Wilma from years back, but she wasn't expecting him. They met up again when she went to Denver. I got the impression he was romantically interested in her. Why else turn up all dressed up on her door step?"

"I don't know what he was after, but it can't be anything good. Look how upset Wilma is. And he seems to have some hold over Mrs. Grey, too, as she just announced they are all traveling to Denver tomorrow. Again." Ellen sobbed. "Mrs. Grey spoke to me like I was a child. I know she speaks to other people like that sometimes but rarely with me."

"Try not to judge until we know all the facts, Ellen, darling. I know you love Wilma but she is an adult."

"But I just...oh, Samuel, what could be so wrong to make her cry like that?" Ellen asked, her voice quivering with emotion.

"I don't know, darling, but come here and give me a hug. We will find out soon enough. In the meantime, we got to think of the children."

Ellen knew her husband was right. She went willingly into his arms and prayed whatever had upset Wilma wouldn't take her away from Clover Springs forever. She meant too much to everyone.

"Wait. Did you say Eleanor was left teaching the school alone?" she asked, an incredulous expression on her face.

"Well, I had to get Wilma..." Samuel said.

"Hi, Miss Ellen," Rosa greeted her as she came in the door. "Why you cuddling Mr. Samuel like that?"

"Afternoon, Rosa. How was school?" Samuel asked.

"It was fun today. Mr. Gary helped Miss Eleanor but she kept going all red. I think she was annoyed with him. But he wasn't doing anything just telling us how lucky we were to have someone as nice as her as a teacher."

Ellen looked at her husband, his eyes dancing with laughter, as he struggled to keep a straight face.

"Did Gary stay the whole time?" Ellen asked.

"Yes, he told us all about London. He used to live there when he was a little boy. He said it's a bit like it was in those stories you read to us by the guy Charles..." Rosa bit her lip trying to remember the authors name.

"Dickens, darling. Yes, I guess it would have changed a bit."

"Where's Wilma? Mr. Gary said she had a 'tin-gushed visitor.'"

Samuel and Ellen laughed. Samuel rubbed Rosa's hair. "You mean a distinguished visitor."

"That's what I said," Rosa insisted.

"Wilma is in the sitting room talking to Father Molloy in private. She will see you later. Can you come and help me with dinner, please?"

"Yes, Miss Ellen."

CHAPTER 41

They fed the children first so the adults could eat and talk in private. The children must have picked up on the atmosphere as they were very quiet, not at all like their usual chatty selves. Ellen longed to tell them they didn't have anything to worry about but she couldn't. Not when she didn't know what was going on. She bit her lip continuously looking at the sitting room door but there was no sign of Wilma or Father Molloy. She kept dinner as long as she could but if they didn't come soon it risked being spoiled.

A knock on the back door announced Mrs. Grey with Zack following in her wake. Laura and Paul were with her, too, their presence not helping Ellen's sense of panic. Laura was ill and should be resting at home. What was she doing here?

"I asked Laura and Paul to join us as Wilma has a story to tell. It is best if Laura hears if firsthand as Wilma won't want to repeat it. I would ask you all to have patience and listen to Wilma. It will be painful but we all have to be brave," Mrs. Grey said trying to smile, but it didn't work. She rubbed a tear away from her eye while Ellen stared at her. She couldn't believe Mrs. Grey was so emotional in front of others. This was a side of her they rarely saw.

"Ellen, darling, please stop looking at Zack as if he was the devil himself. He is part of Wilma's story but in a good way," Mrs. Grey said before smiling at Ellen.

Ellen felt Samuel's arm sneak around her waist.

"I apologize for my wife's reaction. She is very fond of Wilma, and given Wilma's recent illness, she is also very protective. She didn't mean it personally, did you darling?"

Everyone stared at Ellen. She swallowed hard before looking Zack in the eyes.

"I apologize, Mr. Zack. I may have jumped to conclusions," Ellen said apologetically.

"It's Zack and there are no apologies necessary. I am heartened to see how many friends my Wilma has and—"

He was interrupted by Wilma opening the door of the kitchen, Father Molloy following behind.

"I ain't your Wilma."

"I know you aren't yet, but I hope you will be soon," Zack added softly.

Ellen wasn't sure Wilma or anyone else heard him.

"Thank you for being here. Ellen has made dinner and we've kept her waiting long enough. We eat first and then we talk." Wilma's tone told them not to try arguing.

"Paul and I have eaten so we will wait with the children. Call us when you are ready," Laura said before almost running out the door. Ellen wished she could follow her. She wasn't hungry and was certain anything she tried to eat would stick in her throat.

The meal passed in silence. Judging by the amount of food left on the serving plates, Ellen wasn't the only one to lose their appetite. She quickly cleared away the leftover food. It wouldn't go to waste, not with so many children around. She put the water on to boil for the coffee and checked on the children. Tilly had come over from Reverend Timmons's house to help put the children to bed as she always did. Ellen asked some of the older children to help her and instructed the rest of them not to enter the kitchen. She quickly explained that the adults needed to speak in private. She called Laura and Paul back to the kitchen.

"Is something bad going to happen, Miss Ellen?" Rosa asked quietly.

"No, darling. I promise it has nothing to do with

the orphanage. You are all safe here," Ellen reassured them.

The guilt hit her in waves as one by one the children relaxed. The poor little darlings had been so worried and she hadn't tried to reassure them. What type of mother was she?

CHAPTER 42

"Thank you all for coming this evening. I know you were all worried by my tears earlier but I is fine now. Or at least I will be," Wilma reassured them. She looked at Zack, who came to sit beside her. He put his arm around her and she was grateful for his support. Father Molloy sat on her other side.

"This man is Zack. We met some years ago and then more recently in Denver," Wilma explained. She told them her story and that of her daughter and granddaughters. When she finished, the room was deathly silent apart from the occasional sniffle.

"Oh, Wilma, you poor dear, you have been through horrors," Laura said, sniffing back tears.

"Yes, Laura. I hope you don't hold it against me for

not telling you. I just couldn't bear to speak of my daughter."

Laura got up and went over to kiss Wilma on the cheek. "I will never hold anything against you. You are as close to me as any mother could be. I love you. I just wish you got to see Solace before..."

Wilma gulped. She didn't want to break down again. The time for tears was later, in private. "Thank you, sweetheart. I will see her again when the time comes but now I need to go to Denver. I want to bring my grandbabies home."

"What ages are the girls?" Samuel asked.

"Coming up for seven. They are such sweet children, too, although rather quiet. But I guess you can't blame them. Not after all they have been through," Zack explained.

"Why didn't you tell Wilma the story when she was in Denver? She could have met the children then," Ellen said, her suspicious tone making Wilma's eyes widen.

"Ellen, this man has reunited me with my family. Years ago, he saved my life and the cost to him was horrific. Please don't use that tone."

"Sorry, Wilma, Zack. I'm afraid all the upset today has caused me to forget my manners," Ellen apologized again.

"It's quite all right and it's a fair question. I had my

suspicions when Wilma came to Denver. I recognized her from years ago and then when she told her story it reminded me of a story my ex-wife had told me. Solace had changed her name to Sarah but she was found not too far from the plantation Wilma had been living on. There were a lot of unanswered questions. Rather than risk breaking Wilma's heart again, I wanted to be sure before I said anything."

"You did right. We can't thank you enough for what you have done for our Wilma," Father Molloy added quietly. "But why not bring the children with you?"

"I didn't want to raise their hopes as they have been through so much already. I was almost one hundred percent certain Wilma would want them but..."

"There is no question about me wanting them," Wilma interrupted sharply. "Both of them are my flesh and blood. I am going to bring them home and never let them out of my sight again. Ever."

"Well, we might have something to say about that, Wilma. At their age, they should be in school." Laura's comment made them laugh and helped reduce the tension a little.

"So what about you, Zack, what are your plans?"

"Trust you, Mrs. Grey, to be so direct. I am sure that is between Wilma and Zack," Paul Kelley protested.

"I don't mind answering. Thing is, I have never been able to get Wilma out of my head. Not since that time I gave her the cup of water. She was so brave and so beautiful."

"Stop it, you is talking rubbish."

"No, Wilma, it's true. Every word. I tried to find you but it was impossible. I met my wife and got married but it was doomed to failure from the start. We split up a while back. Then I heard of Clara, Eliza Jane's mother's mission to reunite slaves, so I thought that would be a good place to be. Someday, maybe Wilma would come looking for someone."

"You mean you was waiting for me? All that time?"

"Sure was. I am a patient man." Zack sent Wilma a look filled with love.

Ellen coughed. "Maybe the rest of us should retire to the sitting room and leave Wilma and Zack to talk?"

"Let them go to the living room. I need more coffee. And some cookies," Father Molloy exclaimed making everyone but Wilma and Zack laugh. They were too engrossed in each other to notice. Father Molloy tapped Wilma gently on the arm, but she was so shocked she almost leaped out of her skin.

"What do you do that for?"

"You were too busy staring into your man's eyes you didn't hear our plans. Go on, the two of you. We are busy in here and you obviously need to talk," Father Molloy ordered.

Flustered, Wilma got up and went into the sitting room without saying another word. Zack followed but as he reached the kitchen door he turned back.

"I just want to reassure you that I love Wilma with all my heart and never would do anything to hurt her. I am overwhelmed by how much love you have all shown for her. It is quite something to see, especially given the difference in our races."

"We don't see color or race here, only human beings," Father Molloy answered.

"I wish the whole world was like that, Father." With that Zack closed the door.

CHAPTER 43

Ellen handed out hankies to Laura and Mrs. Grey while Paul boiled more water for fresh coffee. Father Molloy was the first to speak. "Do you want some company on your trip to Denver, Mrs. Grey?"

"Yes, please, Father. I would like to introduce you to someone very special to me. A man called Sammy and his family."

"Mrs. Grey, don't tell us you have a new man in your life as well," Samuel said teasingly.

Ellen watched as Mrs. Grey's face turned pink from the base of her neck to the tips of her ears.

"Samuel Higgins mind your manners," Mrs. Grey spluttered. "Sammy was a slave on my father's planation."

Ellen nearly stopped breathing. "You owned slaves?"

"No, but my father did. It's not something I am happy about, but I guess it's time it was out in the open."

"Does he not hate you? After all, your family kept him and his family as property," Ellen asked not wanting to hurt Mrs. Grey, but her curiosity getting the better of her.

"I think Mrs. Grey may have been somewhat involved in his escape," Father Molloy added.

"Wilma told you already." Mrs. Grey looked at Father Molloy in disbelief.

"No, dear Mrs. Grey, Wilma hasn't said a word. I suspected for a long time you had been involved somehow with the Underground Railway. You come from the south yet your attitude is a lot different to that of your contemporaries. Little Beaver adores you and he is a good judge of character."

"He does?"

"Yes, he does and so do we. Now where is that coffee, Paul Kelley?" Father Molloy asked. "I am dying of thirst over here."

Ellen sat down because, if she hadn't, she would have fallen over. Today was a day for shocks. No two ways about it. Only then did she remember Eleanor.

"I should go check on Eleanor. Rosa said Gary helped teach school today," Ellen said.

"Yes he did. I happened to be at the school when young Tilly came to get me. Gary was helping her and from what I could see they got on just fine."

"Is that a twinkle in your eye, Father Molloy? You wouldn't be doing a bit of matchmaking now, would you?"

"I am a Catholic priest, Ellen Higgins. We don't do matchmaking."

"And I am the Queen of England."

Ellen's retort made them all laugh. Samuel leaned over and kissed her on the cheek. She was lucky to live among such wonderful people. Would Gary and Eleanor be the next couple to get wed in Clover Springs or would Zack and Wilma beat them to the altar?

CHAPTER 44

Later that evening, Gary and Eleanor called to the orphanage. Mrs. Grey introduced them to Zack and told them why he had come to Clover Springs. In turn, Eleanor told everyone present about her past. Ellen didn't say a word, she was too overwhelmed by the events of the day.

"Do you think Eliza Jane could help me find my mama? Or maybe some of her family?" Eleanor asked.

"I am sure she could. She will certainly try her best," Zack confirmed.

It was agreed they should all travel to Denver as soon as possible rather than wait for Doc Erin to return. Wilma was keen to meet her grandchildren and Eleanor wanted to ask Eliza Jane personally if she could help her search for her family. Gary insisted on going with Eleanor so Samuel offered to mind the saloon.

"Don't take too much notice of Murph. He just likes to talk," Gary warned him.

"Murph would be better doing more praying and less drinking," Father Molloy muttered.

"Are you still coming to Denver, Father Grumpy?" Mrs. Grey asked making everyone laugh.

"I will, if you behave yourself, Mrs. Grey." The priest's response resulted in more laughter.

It was decided they would travel at the weekend. Ellen and Laura would share teaching duty to allow Eleanor time to go to Denver.

* * *

On the train, Eleanor sat beside Gary, her hand entwined in his. She still couldn't believe just how much her life had changed since coming to Clover Springs. Not only had she found a wonderful man who loved her and offered her a future, but she had found real friends. These people totally accepted her for who she was. And just to add to everything, they had vowed to help her find her mama. Maybe her mama was dead but she could have other family, brothers or sisters, maybe nieces and nephews.

She looked with fondness at Wilma. If she found

her mama, she would love her to be like the older woman. Wilma sat beside Zack, her face a mixture of delight and apprehension. Wilma was worried how her two grandchildren would react to her. She was also dealing with the grief of Solace's death. It was one thing assuming your child was dead, it was another having it confirmed.

Mrs. Grey smiled at her as Eleanor's gaze reached her. She had told them all about Sammy and how he had taught her how to care for horses. He'd been one of her father's most valuable slaves but Mrs. Grey hadn't hesitated to help him escape all those years ago. Sammy had a family now and had insisted Mrs. Grey get to know them all. He was adamant, they wouldn't exist but for her actions when she was younger. Eleanor thought Mrs. Grey was so brave. It was one thing for a slave to run away, they had to try to gain their freedom. But for a white woman to go against her family and her society, that took real courage. She wished David, the US doctor Mrs. Grey had loved had survived the war too.

"Do you think Wilma's grandchildren will come back to Clover Springs with her, Mrs. Grey?"

"I certainly hope so but who knows. Those poor children have been through an awful lot already."

"We need to convince them. Everyone should move to Clover Springs," Jane said with conviction making the others laugh. Eleanor squeezed her friend's hand. She had really bonded with Jane and was hoping she would settle in the small town. She was returning to Denver to see her family and also Reverend Douglass. Wilma was still hopeful the young couple would be able to get past the trauma of Jane's attack at the hands of some white boys.

"What will happen to Rosa and John if Wilma has her grandchildren living with her? Won't they get upset?"

Mrs. Grey's facial expression told Eleanor she shared her concern but she made no comment. Eleanor guessed the older woman didn't think the train was the right place to discuss it.

She was probably right. She settled back in the hard seat trying to get comfortable. She might as well try and get some sleep. It would be hours before they reached their destination.

CHAPTER 45

Mrs. Grey had booked them all into the same hotel as the one she and Wilma had used on their last trip. Eleanor couldn't help thinking she did that on purpose to upset the hotel manager who seemed to believe black people should stay at different accommodation. But he was enough of a businessman to accept the large booking and the resulting amount of dollars. Eleanor liked her hotel room. She had offered to share with Jane but her friend preferred to go home and stay with her aunt, Eliza Jane. Zack was also staying at his home, leaving Father Molloy, Wilma, Mrs. Grey, herself and Gary to stay at the hotel.

Father Molloy had gone for a walk to find the nearby church. Wilma had claimed tiredness and had gone to lie down. Eleanor understood the older woman needed to prepare herself for meeting her grandchildren. Gary had gone with Zack to bring Jane home. That left Mrs. Grey and Eleanor to enjoy afternoon tea.

"Are you glad you came to Denver Eleanor?"

'Yes Mrs. Grey. Wilma thinks some of these people may be able to help me find my mama's family. Of course I've been told she is dead but maybe that was another lie."

"It could very well be the case. There was a lot of heartache surrounding that period, on all sides." Mrs. Grey looked pensive. "War isn't black and white. There were good and bad fighting for both the North and South."

"But you are glad the North won aren't you?

"I am but with reservations. If you spend a little time in Denver, you will see life for our black friends isn't a bed of roses," Mrs. Grey said sadly. "They are not treated as equals. Until the world sees people for who they are rather than their nationality, color or religion, we will never have won anything." Mrs. Grey stirred her coffee, her mind miles away.

Eleanor stayed quiet not wanting to interrupt the other woman.

"I am sorry Eleanor, I find it hard seeing how Sammy and his family are living. Yet he thinks he is comfortable."

"Well if he is happy and healthy Mrs. Grey isn't that a good thing? You can't rescue everyone. Not even you and Wilma are that good."

Mrs. Grey smiled at Eleanor, her kind eyes lit up. "You are a very sensible young lady, Eleanor. A real credit to your family even though they are too bigoted to see it."

"Mrs. Grey, what do you think will happen? Do you think Wilma's grandchildren will come back with us? Will she marry Zack?"

Mrs. Grey laughed out loud.

"Who knows child what Wilma will do about Zack. I can't imagine our Wilma playing the role of a little housewife but then there is a real connection between her and Zack. I guess time will tell. As for the grandchildren, yes I think Wilma will bring them home with her. Once she sees them, she won't ever let them go."

"Why does that make you sad?"

"Sad? I am not sad, Eleanor, at least not for Wilma and her family. It's wonderful and I am thrilled for my friend. She deserves to be happy. I am just a little concerned about the effect on Rosa and John. They look on her as a granny. They may feel a bit pushed out. I know Wilma will do her best not to let that happen but..."

Eleanor didn't get a chance to reply as Gary walked into the dining room.

"What are my two favorite ladies talking about? Me I hope?"

"Go away with you Mr. Barrett. Favorite lady indeed. You barely knew my name last month." Mrs. Grey stood up, smoothing down her dress, her smile showing them she was teasing. "I am going to lie down for a bit. I will see you two later."

EPILOGUE

"Doc Erin is coming home. She wanted to know if we would still be here in Denver when she gets here," Wilma said stirring her coffee. "I guess that depends on my girls."

Mrs. Grey nodded before asking "Are Doc Erin and everyone else all well?"

"She doesn't say. She just says she has a lot of news for us."

"Not half as much as we have for her," Mrs. Grey smiled at Wilma. "Seems like a year since she left, yet it's only been about a month. I wonder why they had to stay in New York for so long?"

Wilma didn't get a chance to answer.

"I am sure they will tell us when they get back," Mrs. Grey said. "After we tell them all the news from here. Especially about you getting married." Mrs. Grey looked up from her coffee to study Wilma's face.

"Mrs. Grey, don't start that again. I didn't say I was going to marry Zack."

"Yes, you did, you just didn't put it into words. You love him and he loves you. When we get back from Denver, we have us a wedding to plan. Your grandchildren can be flower girls."

"Can you believe how nice the girls are? I have to pinch myself."

Mrs. Grey smiled, knowing how much finding her family meant to Wilma. She looked up as there was a knock on the door. Gary came in followed closely by Eleanor.

"Mrs. Grey, Miss Wilma, sorry for interrupting you but we have something we want to ask you."

"Yes, Gary," Wilma replied.

Gary took Eleanor's hand. "We wanted to tell you we are getting married as soon as we get back to Clover Springs. Wilma, we would like you to give Eleanor away."

Wilma stood up so quickly she knocked over her coffee. She didn't seem to care but took Eleanor into her arms and hugged her close.

"Thank you, Wilma, for helping me see the light," Eleanor said.

"You are welcome, child. You two is going to be very happy together."

"Actually, we are hoping to become four," Eleanor said giving Gary a quick look. He nodded in approval.

Mrs. Grey saw Wilma looked as confused as she felt.

"I am not sure what you mean?" Wilma's gaze slipped to Eleanor's stomach causing the girl to turn scarlet.

"Oh no, not… It's just…"

"What my darling, stammering bride-to-be is trying to ask is would you consider us as adoptive parents for Rosa and John? After we marry, of course. And preferably, after our honeymoon."

"Gary!" Eleanor chided him.

"Sorry, but I want some time alone with my wife." Gary didn't look a bit sorry.

"Rosa and John? Are you sure?" Mrs. Grey hated herself for asking but she couldn't bear it if those children got hurt again.

Gary put his arm around Eleanor's shoulders.

"Yes, Mrs. Grey, we are sure. I love Rosa. Always have, and Eleanor has fallen for her charms too. We know the children will not be separated so we would like to offer both a home. And a future."

Wilma had yet to speak. She went over to Gary and pulled him into a hug. Then she turned to Eleanor. "I am prouder of you now than I could be of my own daughter. Your mama was a special woman to produce a girl like you. Your father too."

Mrs. Grey smiled at both of them before adding, "Your timing couldn't be better. I didn't say anything to Wilma as I didn't want to give her more to worry about."

"What you not tell me? Is you sick?"

"No, Wilma. I am perfectly healthy." At Wilma's confused expression, Mrs. Grey took her friend's hand before facing Eleanor and Garry once more.

"Wilma's twin granddaughters will be coming to live in Clover Springs. I was concerned Rosa would feel pushed out. But this is the solution to everything."

"I was so caught up in my own happiness, I never thought about how those two young'uns would react.," Wilma said sadly.

"Wilma, you cannot think of everyone all the time," Mrs. Grey reassured her friend.

"They will be so happy to have real parents. Rosa loves you, Gary. And John loves anyone who makes Rosa happy." Wilma clapped her hands together happily.

"Clover Springs has worked another happy ending." Mrs. Grey smiled widely.

"Just wait until Doc Erin comes home and learns

all this. Maybe someone else will get a happy ending?" Wilma said, a teasing note in her voice.

"Like who?" Eleanor asked, her eyes twinkling as Wilma continued to stare at Mrs. Grey.

"Me?" Mrs. Grey protested. "I am too old to get involved in one of your matchmaking schemes, Miss Wilma whatever your surname is."

"Me thinks the lady doth protest too much," Gary quoted.

Eleanor laughed out loud as Mrs. Grey kept protesting and Wilma kept teasing. She didn't know whether Mrs. Grey would get her happy ever after, or if Wilma would say yes to Zack the next time he asked her to marry him. She hoped they would.

Clover Springs had brought her more happiness than she ever thought possible. She was happy, she was surrounded by love and friendship and she had a rosy future to look forward to. Gary turned toward her, to find her staring at him.

"What are you staring at?" he asked, moving closer to her.

"My future," she replied before rising on her tippy toes to kiss him briefly. "I love you Mr. Barrett."

* * *

A BLAST from the past arrives and rocks Mary's happiness in the process. Find out more about Cathy here. Doc Erin brings some friends back to Clover Springs, if you want to find out what she was up to while in New York, click here.

HISTORICAL NOTE

The idea for the characters in this episode in Clover Springs came from two sources.

Eleanor, the new teacher is based, very loosely, on a story I read about a while ago. In London, a double portrait that was commissioned by the 1st Earl of Mansfield circa 1770's hangs in one of the old houses. In it, there are two very fashionably dressed young ladies. Nothing unusual in that. The fashion of the day was to commission double portraits albeit usually of husband and wife, mother and child or sisters. In this case the girls weren't sisters. Also one was white, the other black.

The black woman's name was Dido Elizabeth Belle. Her father was Captain John Lindsay, a nephew of Lord Mansfield. Legend has it, Dido's father met Maria, a slave, on a ship on one of his West Indian trips. Whether they fell in love, he raped her or she willingly traded favors for a better voyage will remain speculation. However, the fact remains when the slave died, Captain Lindsay acknowledged his daughter in so much as he sent her to the UK to be raised as a lady. She benefited from the same lessons provided for her cousin, Lady Elizabeth Murray, the great niece of William Murray.

Lord Mansfield (William Murray) was Lord Chief Justice for 32 years and as such one of the most admired in the 18th Century Britain. He was known for a razor sharp mind, and being fair minded. He was also wealthy, had a title and so was extremely powerful. He was an abolitionist and set the precedent that on English soil, no man was a slave. The case he is most famous for involved the horrific massacre of slaves. The Zong ship was massively overcrowded and when the resulting epidemic broke out, the Captain decided rather than try to save the slaves, he threw at least a third of them overboard. His intent was to claim the insurance on his "cargo." The Captain argued he was being merciful to the other slaves who would benefit from more space and more supplies. Thankfully, Lord Mansfield presided and the insurance company refused to pay out.

Lord Mansfield, who was childless, did his best to protect Belle during his lifetime. He also made provision for her in the event of his death by adding codicil after codicil to his will. By all accounts, he held her in very high esteem.

Reading the above story gave me the inspiration for Eleanor. Her story doesn't share much similarities with Belle, but I thought you might like to know how she came about.

* * *

The second character inspired by a true historical figure is **Eliza Jane** – the former slave who tries to help Wilma find her family.

"Aunt" Clara Brown was a former slave who made it her life's business to find the husband and children she had lost while enduring life as a slave. She'd been sold so often, she had no idea where her four children had gone or if they even lived. Her last "owner's" family set her free on his death sometime in the 1850's.

Before the Civil War, she headed west to Colorado after hearing a rumor her daughter Eliza Jane had gone that way. She was made walk for most of the 700 mile journey as a black person couldn't buy a stage-coach ticket. She couldn't find her daughter in Denver so moved on with some miners to Central City. By working hard, she started to save money to achieve her dream to find her family. She was an excellent business woman and a hard worker and accumulated a fortune - $10,000 by the end of the civil war. She used the money to invest in different properties and businesses.

She travelled all over trying to find her family and in the process brought former slaves to Colorado. She helped those she could regardless of color or religion. She believed in community spirit. She lost a lot of papers in the great flood of Denver in 1864 proving ownership of her assets, her house and several properties were destroyed by fire in Central city in the 1870's yet she kept going.

She finally found her daughter Eliza Jane after many years of searching.

Clara Brown had died by 1888 – the time period of my story and I have no idea whether her daughter continued the search for missing relatives. I just kept thinking of what it would be like to lose my children. I know I would never ever stop looking and it's much easier today with social media.

I thought of how hard Clara Brown had worked not only to find her family but also to help those around her. I like to think her daughter would have helped Wilma had my character been real.

ALSO BY RACHEL WESSON

The Resistance Sisters

Darkness Falls

Light Rises

Hearts at War

When's Mummy Coming

A Mother's Promise

WWII Irish Stand Alone

Stolen from her Mother

Orphans of Hope House

Home for unloved Orphans (Orphans of Hope House 1)

Baby on the Doorstep (Orphans of Hope House 2)

Women and War

Gracie under Fire

Penny's Secret Mission

Molly's Flight

Hearts on the Rails

Orphan Train Escape

Orphan Train Trials

Orphan Train Christmas

Orphan Train Tragedy

Orphan Train Strike

Orphan Train Disaster

Trail of Hearts - Oregon Trail Series

Oregon Bound (book 1)

Oregon Dreams (book 2)

Oregon Destiny (book 3)

Oregon Discovery (book 4)

Oregon Disaster (book 5)

12 Days of Christmas - co -authored series.

The Maid - book 8

Clover Springs Mail Order Brides

Katie (Book 1)

Mary (Book 2)

Sorcha (Book 3)

Emer (Book 4)

Laura (Book 5)

Ellen (Book 6)

Thanksgiving in Clover Springs (book 7)

Christmas in Clover Springs (book8)

Erin (Book 9)

Eleanor (book 10)

Cathy (book 11)

Mrs. Grey

Clover Springs East

New York Bound (book 1)

New York Storm (book 2)

New York Hope (book 3)

ACKNOWLEDGMENTS

These books wouldn't have been possible without the help of so many people. Thanks to Erin Dameron-Hill for my fantastic covers. Erin is a gifted artist who makes my characters come to life.

The ladies from Pioneer Hearts who volunteered to proofread my book. Special thanks go to Marlene Larsen, Cindy Nipper, Janet Lesley, Robin Malek, Meisje Sanders Arcuri and Denise Cervantes who all spotted errors that had slipped through.

Last, but by no means least, huge thanks and love to my husband and my three children.

Come join us at https://www.facebook.com/groups/rachelwessonsreaders

Printed in Great Britain
by Amazon

61598989R00190